Alice Frank

Stepping through the centuries

**A door in time enables two friends to explore life in
Altrincham, Stockport and Bowdon across three centuries**

Alice Frank

Alice Frank

Stepping
through the
centuries

A door in time enables two friends to explore life in
Altrincham, Stockport and Bowdon across three centuries

Alice Frank

Stepping through the centuries

A door in time enables two friends to explore life in Altrincham, Stockport and Bowdon across three centuries

MEMOIRS

Cirencester

Alec Frank

Stepping through the centuries

A door in time enables two friends to explore life in
Altrincham, Stockport and Bowdon across three centuries

MEMOIRS
Cirencester

MEMOIRS
PUBLISHING

1A The Wool Market Dyer Street Cirencester Gloucestershire GL7 2PR
An imprint of Memoirs Publishing www.mereobooks.com

Stepping through the centuries: 978-1-86151-328-1

First published in Great Britain in 2017
by Mereo Books, an imprint of Memoirs Publishing

The address for Memoirs Publishing Group Limited can be found at
www.memoirspublishing.com

The Memoirs Publishing Group Ltd Reg. No. 7834348

The Memoirs Publishing Group supports both The Forest Stewardship Council® (FSC®) and the
PEFC® leading international forest-certification organisations. Our books carrying both the FSC
label and the PEFC® and are printed on FSC®-certified paper. FSC® is the only
forest-certification scheme supported by the leading environmental organisations including
Greenpeace. Our paper procurement policy can be found at
www.memoirspublishing.com/environment

Typeset in 11/16pt Goudy
by Wiltshire Associates Publisher Services Ltd. Printed and bound in Great Britain by
Printondemand-Worldwide, Peterborough PE2 6XD

When two girls find a mysterious house concealed under an ancient tree on the Devisdale in Bowdon, they discover that the cellar steps can take them back in time to the London of 1665, the year of the Great Plague. It proves to be the first of many visits to the house and to the plague-ridden capital, and they soon find themselves witnessing the Great Fire of London, which follows the Plague the next year.

After nursing the victims of the Plague, Jessica becomes a dedicated nurse, starting off as a cadet at Altrincham Hospital and then training at Stepping Hill and St Thomas's in Stockport, and then back to Bowdon Maternity Hospital, then called Southfields. As the girls grow older and explore further, their travels through time and their encounters with people from the 17th century give them much to think about, including the ways attitudes to social care, mental health, nursing practice and tenancy law have changed.

CONTENTS

By the same author

A Bowdon Romance
A Dangerous Obsession

INTRODUCTION

In 1959, when this story is set, I was 15 like Jessica and Peggy. Many things have got better since then, because we do progress through the years, yet it always seems to be two steps forward and one back. For example, I think we are now much nearer to getting the correct balance in protecting landlords and tenants from one another. In my grandmother's day, the landlord could put the rent up until it was impossible for the tenant to pay it any more, and then he'd be chucked out. My great aunts would tell me how they would see whole families evicted; they'd be sitting in the road with all their belongings. They wouldn't have been given so much as a week's notice, maybe none at all. On top of this, even if they were able to pay a very high rent, the conditions they were living in would be appalling.

In my era all that had gone, but we had moved to the other extreme. One woman was sent to prison for contempt of court because she had evicted someone after having failed to get a court order. Yet the house was in such poor condition she had to go out to work to keep the tenant. The tenant, meanwhile, had so much money that she didn't have to go out to work. She had the flat upstairs, which was the biggest part of the house, while the landlady was crammed into two rooms downstairs. It wasn't until it was reported in the newspapers that neighbours realised who was the landlady and who was the tenant. They had seen the tenant travelling around in her big flash car, very well dressed and clearly quite moneyed, and the landlady going out to work in a factory, very shabbily dressed.

There was so much publicity about it that the tenant had to go. Maybe she was shamed into it; maybe thugs started throwing stones at her windows in the name of caring. This sort of thing happens when there is a lot of publicity about someone. Anything for an excuse to throw stones.

Buying to let is putting up the prices of houses, yet there is still a need for some private landlords, and it's difficult to find a better system.

Drugs were virtually unheard of in the 1950s. I was in Italy in 1965 when I had a letter from my mother saying, "I think there is going to be a big drug problem, I don't think it's just newspaper talk, your sister has come across it in her own social life." These days there can't be anyone who hasn't had some personal experience of drugs. I had no idea how much we would all be affected by it in one way or another, for example, having to keep our houses very securely locked up.

Another big difference between today and 1959 is that houses are so much warmer. Central heating is now taken for granted. It used to be agony getting up in the morning. A woman would take her bra to work and put it on in the toilet there; it would be so cold next to your skin at home. When you got home at night you would dread going from the sitting room to the kitchen, as it would be freezing cold in the hall, and then when you went to bed again at night the sheets would be like ice. We would use hot water bottles, or an electric blanket if we could afford one. Having said all this, there are still some very cold houses. When I go inside them they take me right back to the 1950s.

People find it unbelievable when I tell them how easy it was to get a job in those days, that when I was 16, I went to the Labour Exchange in Moss Lane, Altrincham, to put my name down for work, then walked over the bridge and into a factory called Cook's to ask them if anything was going and got a job straight away. I went straight back to the Labour Exchange and told them to take my name off the list. It is quite realistic in my story that Charmaine gave up her job in Woolworths one week and started another one in a record shop the next. I have sometimes wondered if it's because it's more difficult for firms to sack people these days that it's also become more difficult to get them to employ you in the first place.

I left school at 15 and had various jobs. My parents let me do this, and in between they would pay for me to have lessons in English, arithmetic or history. They did with me what they are trying to do in schools today – keeping the kids studying, but at the same time sending them out on work experience.

One thing they have certainly progressed in is medicine. I have spoken quite a bit about Queenie, who lived next door to the post office in the 1950s, ranting and raving away at anyone walking past her house. She was hallucinating and behaving as though she was drunk. To use the words of those days, they came and put her away. They kept her in for about nine months. They were trying her out on medication. Progress was being made and they were full of hope that they would find something that would cure her. I am afraid they didn't.

She didn't have such a dreadful time when she was inside. In fact she said to the postman when she came out, "I saw your wife in Altrincham. She did look tired, she looked like she needed a holiday". Then she started talking about Parkside, the place where she had been, and telling the postman he should take his wife away there for a holiday.

The phrase 'put away' is now very old fashioned, because this is no longer what happens. It used to be that you would keep seeing someone in the street, shouting and clearly not right, and one day he would just disappear, to be looked after for the rest of his life. These days, quite often someone will only disappear for a while, and then they are seen walking down the road again. They may look a bit shaken, an eye may have to be kept on them for a while, but it is no longer a case of someone never being seen again because they were 'put away'.

It amuses me how meanings of word can change. In the 1880s there was a Lunacy Commissioner. The word was accepted by patients in those days, even welcome. The patients would be very pleased to see the Lunacy Commissioner arriving inside the hospital, coming to see to all their needs. Of course these days he would be called the Mental Health Commissioner.

In 1898 my grandfather was 19 and would play cricket on a green that backed onto a mental hospital. The patients would come out and watch them play. If he played badly they would shout across to him, "Oy, you should be in here with us!" That's all I know about it, but it doesn't sound to me as though they were locked up or in any way being intimidated.

In my book A Dangerous Obsession I wrote about the exceptions and malpractice. I do know that doctors and social workers as a rule are dedicated and very efficient, but it still remains very difficult to complain about them or to get notes corrected without endangering yourself – I can't see any progress there. Even if it is accepted that there is such a thing as malpractice, it will still be referred to as very rare, and great emphasis will be put on the word "very". I think people are frightened of these professionals, and will say things in the face of any documentary evidence to contradict them or even refuse to look at it.

It seems that the interest of the government ministers is to defend the staff and not to protect the patients. They seem to refuse to accept that they are only human, a cross-section of people, and it won't be all that unusual for things to go very wrong. In fact it has reminded some people of how the clergy had to be treated in Ireland. They are infallible. Another example is the late Sir Jimmy Savile. The lord of the manor can do no wrong.

The medical profession and social services may be the same as any other profession – you can find corruption in them all – but it seems they are the only ones where you can't complain about what they do. For example, if a solicitor doesn't put your name on the land register when you buy a house or if he hasn't got a certificate to practice, you can go to the Law Society about it. They will look into it and at the same time you will be perfectly safe. You won't have anyone knocking on your door saying this isn't normal behaviour and they are coming to "take care" of you.

If someone maliciously telephones the RSPCA and says you are ill-treating a dog, you have nothing to worry about. They have got to see the dog. They can't say you have one if you haven't.

In a school a teacher is never 'late', he/she has been 'delayed', and nor do they ever lose anything – they say it has been 'mislaid'. But at least they admit to that and most certainly they don't take it out on the kids. People are not to think it's the same in every profession, I once heard a solicitor say, "the police would have a man doing time rather than admit to it that they got the wrong one convicted" and I most certainly have plenty to suggest that it's the same in social services. They would have someone put on a section rather than have to correct their notes and admit to it that the social worker wrote them all wrong.

At the time of writing, HMRC (previously the Inland Revenue) is trying to get the power to look into anyone's bank account, but there has been an outcry about it. Some people are saying, for example accountants, that some of them won't have an interest in collecting in the taxes – it will be to get control and nothing else. There may even be malice. This is accepted. People need protecting.

It is a dreadful shame that there are not the same safeguards in the Mental Health Act before a compulsory admission into hospital. That is if it's for assessment purposes under a Section 2. They have to say they believe that a person is either a danger to themselves or someone else, and it is something that can be said far too easily on false pretences. The trouble here is that they may find something very easy to believe, just from bias, for example if they think that patient might complain about them.

There has been publicity about some of these carers living in an atmosphere of fear and bullying one another into submission, yet at times it seems that some officials who are quite high up do it to one another as well. A whole team can go wrong. It takes three health officials to have someone certified, but people can work one another up. They can even sometimes get together in a crowd and pick on one person, and you can get some pretty bitchy behaviour in some of these offices.

It's quite serious for the patients that Government ministers seem to think a mental health team would be exempt from anything like this. Yet in fact we are all human and it can be bad enough even when it's the norm. The mental health team is scrupulous, trying to be independent, if all three need to go by the same history, for example.

It is quite different from a person being held on remand or on grounds of suspicion. This comes under completely different legislation and is not to be confused with the powers of the Mental Health Act, and although I am aware that there is trouble from time to time about the police making up information, it is not a thing they can easily do. The rules are very strict about them having correct information, and in the case of someone suspected of crime, how long they can hold someone for; 96 hours is the maximum without either charging or releasing them and even then it can only be for 12 to 24 hours at a time. They have to keep applying for extensions, and meanwhile they have to be gathering evidence, and they have to try to get it right.

In a mental hospital it can be as long as 28 days before a patient can be heard at a tribunal and insist that the facts about their case are correct, to make it clear that allegations against them are unfounded. It seems that a psychiatric patient is a second-class citizen; there would be all hell to pay if the police held anyone as long as that on fabricated evidence.

It's the same with customs officers when you're travelling abroad. They can't have a person detained just because someone has said they have cigarettes inside their suitcase. The customs officers have to look and see them too, as most people would expect. I believe that only if it comes under the Mental Health Act can they simply go by hearsay or even according to what any idiot has told them, and I want to emphasize the word "idiot". It is idiots who make these malicious phone calls and it is very serious for the patients that there's nothing in the Mental Health Act to say that if they are going to act upon a claim, then they've also got to try to investigate it.

The Mental Health Act was revised in 2007, but this point was left unchanged. I realised years later when I got involved in a case of rape that it wasn't this so much that concerned me, maybe very little, but that it showed how much the government ministers were in denial, and I knew how very dangerous that can get. In this case of rape, although it became obvious that the woman was making it all up out of spite, it was also obvious what the difficulty was. Women are in great need of protection from this, but men are also in need of protection from women who will just invent claims, and it's difficult to keep the correct balance. It wasn't that the police were in any way bent and no one was saying that either all men or all women were infallible, as seems to be the case here. That is as regards the government ministers and the mental health team. If anyone has a better explanation, I would love to hear it.

Any changes they did make to the Mental Health Act were made after the patient had been put into a mental hospital and it was too late. For example, they'd be able to see a mental health advocate. The government made no attempt to change it to say that they should be found not guilty before being certified, even when there was plenty of parliamentary time. It wasn't that we were making steady progress and time ran out – we never made any progress at all. We couldn't even get them to understand what the request was. It seemed they had a blind spot. It was more than careless, it was reckless – they were left with a great deal of power to maintain their opinions, especially if they said their interest was to "look after" someone.

The Human Rights Act now gives patients a good deal of protection from this, including cases where they make the claim that their interest is to help the patient, but the Mental Health Act is the main body of legislation. In any case we don't know how long it is going to remain in force now that we are coming out of Europe. If it is going to be replaced by the British Bill of Rights I can't see this government protecting the patients in the same way.

Of course there are times when a patient has to be told that they are not in there to be punished and that the staff have a duty of care towards them, but it can get completely out of control and can be done far too easily on false pretences. Yet despite all the documentary evidence to show this, the ministers would be almost confirming it, as they would talk as though the mental health team were infallible and send out standard fobbing-off letters which were probably printed out by the dozen. Some people said it was their way of saying that they were so perfect they wouldn't let such a thing happen in any case, so this safeguard wouldn't be needed. This frightened them very much. It is a very serious step to take, to use force when saying you know better than someone else how they should be looking after themselves or whether or not they are some kind of danger. Yet despite all the protests and proposals, they refused to stipulate that opinions have to be based on facts. The mental health team don't have to try to get it right, it's left to trust.

The Department of Health even gave a guarantee; they stated that three health officials would have to sign, which would ensure that all circumstances would be looked into. People were gobsmacked. One woman exclaimed "Bollocks!" I think she felt insulted after all the evidence she had sent in to the contrary and wanted to insult them back.

The Government ministers were contradicted by psychologists on this point. People sent in quotes from psychology books on how people can get together in a crowd and work one another up, but they got no response; probably the ministers didn't even look at them. There's no simple explanation. It isn't an easy way of getting someone inside for an assessment, or that it may be an emergency and there isn't the time to investigate it, nor is there something simple and straightforward somewhere else. Sometimes we have to settle for it; things can happen, and it's very strange. It seems the ministers are in complete denial.

It is also very strange the way anyone else can get it, any Tom, Dick or Harry. You can go into any pub, talk to anyone and they will show you how they have understood. They will say things like, "You should be found not guilty before you are convicted, not after." Unlike the ministers, that's without seeing any of the documentary evidence there is to support it. Why is it only those with power who can't get it? There's some common factor.

Maybe we would have given in much sooner if we had suspected so strongly then that this was the issue. Maybe an analogy is appropriate. If someone is a terrible thief there's no stopping them if he or she is a heroin addict, and it seems that there is no stopping Government Ministers either. They are in denial, and this is the root of the problem. Yet we did persevere.

They also failed to see the difference between fact and opinion. I'll say it again: there would be the most dreadful outcry if the police couldn't differentiate, made a statement that a man had committed a burglary, acted upon it, and it was merely an opinion based on anyone's say so, but when people just cannot get the point and won't answer the question you are left to draw up your own conclusions, and this is why I have concluded that in the case of psychiatry the problem is a combination of the patients being second-class citizens and the staff being infallible.

My mind has sometimes gone back to 1959, when I was in the USA and witnessed people's attitude towards the blacks. It was as though they had no voice, the way I was told to ignore them, and it seems to be the same in psychiatry. Just as long as someone has some sort of a history or is speaking on their behalf then you can say anything about them, and you will be especially covered if you make the claim at the same time that your interest in it is to "help" them.

I think there is also the problem that we are indoctrinated into thinking we should care about one another. It is something we are taught from when we're very young and is considered admirable, consequently there comes a time when it can be used as an excuse by anyone at all, and not just mental health teams. For example a neighbour might have been a witness to something but is afraid to speak out, afraid of what she may get involved in if she tries to defend the patient. It is an easy way out to say that it doesn't matter as the patient will be so well "looked after". People can be very good at believing what they want to. They may even convince themselves that this is in their interests too and this is why they're doing it. All this will not only make them look very caring, it will ensure they are covered by the Mental Health Act.

I have had first-hand experience of a case where a relative was phoning everyone up and blatantly asking questions about someone's will. The social worker argued that his interest was in that person's welfare, and not in the money. That came to no surprise to a psychologist, as the drive to get control can be very strong. Yet at one time it seemed that our protests against it were being used as evidence against us. When we cried out "Take care, some people will say that this is in the patient's interests when really it's to get control" and enclosed documentary evidence to support us, instead of making certain that this amendment was put into the Mental Health Act, they started discussing what further power to give mental health staff if the person concerned is unable to understand that their interest is to "help" them. It reminded me of the psychologist Irvin Goffman, who called it "looping" in a book called Asylum. He said: "The very thing you say to try to prove your case is used to undo you and prove that your opponent is right."

Another reply I had when referring to the Mental Health Act said: "If the person disagrees with the reasons given, there is no legal way under current law of challenging this before admission. After admission a person can apply to a Mental Health Review, which gives them an opportunity to put their "views" [my inverted commas] to an independent body."

This is just one example among so many which shows how they couldn't understand that we were not talking about bad judgement or different opinions; our only interest was that a person should not be found guilty of an incident they hadn't committed.

In another answer we were told "Other than for a very short time, the use of compulsory powers has to be sanctioned by an independent tribunal which will take evidence from the person concerned."

As I keep saying, it would be considered very serious if it happened to someone anywhere else; he or she was held for days at a time, maybe as many as 28, before they were able to do more than put their evidence forward, but they could also insist that it was looked at, and 28 days would be considered a very long time.

In fact it is also a very long time for a psychiatric patient, and a lot of damage can be done in that time, especially if the patient is already vulnerable. As one person put it, "If you're not mad when you go in, you're mad when you come out". There may also be a problem if they have had pressure put on them to take medication. It's not unusual for it to have side effects and most certainly it should not be taken unnecessarily. But when we wrote to the Minister of Health about it, emphasizing that we wanted it in the Mental Health Act that opinions should be based on factual evidence BEFORE a compulsory admission (not after), and making it clear that 28 days was far too long to have to wait, they yet again gave us a shocking reply and yet again we saw how blind they were. Incredibly so; they could only read it as a complaint about the delays after a patient had rightly been found guilty.

They said, "We know there have been problems in the past with patients having to wait a long time for their tribunal hearing. That is why there was a recruitment campaign for the recruitment of further members to the tribunals, which has had some success. The situation regarding delays and postponements is now a lot better than it was a year ago." They just couldn't get the point that the patient shouldn't be there in the first place accused of an incident for which they had not been responsible. Maybe most extraordinary is that they managed to make this interpretation, and we didn't even know about the postponements. It was the first we'd heard of them. There comes a time when you have to accept that someone isn't going to understand.

It is true that the patient has to be showing other symptoms of a mental illness, maybe the mad look in the eye or walking as though they're drunk, but how easy they may all find it to see if they are all biased about the same thing. They may find it especially easy to see if that patient is vulnerable.

In any case, even if the person is showing other symptoms and it isn't just health officials making it up, how can they make judgement on whether or not it matters, and whether or not they have the right to go inside that person's house and take them away, if the claims against them have not been looked into? It may tip the balance of the scales dramatically if the facts about their case are wrong. There are quite a few people walking about who may behave oddly but are of no danger to themselves or anyone else. It isn't usually people with mental health problems who commit violent crimes, but it may be they who would be most damaged by anything like this.

It is also true that before a person is committed they have to be interviewed. Might they make that person angry or even frightened during the interview with some of their allegations, so they can then say that the person was behaving like a madman – ie have other symptoms of mental illness?

The idea of the interview may be that it gives them a chance to tell their side of the story, but the professionals don't have to believe it; maybe we can give it as an example of Irvin Goffman's "looping", as it can be used as evidence against them. Without investigating, they can say it's paranoiac. For example if a person says he has a stalker, they can refuse to listen to reliable witnesses before a compulsory admission into hospital, regardless of how easily they could do so, and so much can go by hearsay. There can also sometimes be a very thin line between going by hearsay and actually making up information, and the only time the patient can insist that it's investigated is when they are being held on a section.

In any case the interview doesn't have to take long. One mental health charity said when putting this proposal forward that there should be factual evidence: "The common experience is that the assessment is still often based on a relatively short interview with the person cared for and this can be by professionals who have never met him/her before."

In fact one person who had been sectioned told me there had been no social worker present. When I found out that in fact there had been, she said, "I thought he was a plain-clothes police officer. He hardly spoke to me once, he spent all the time in the next room talking to the police". Whether or not it's true, one thing is certain – it all too easily could be, and it did look as though much of it had gone by hearsay.

They can also refuse to look at letters said to have been written by the patient and used as evidence. They can take the complainant's word for what they say or even if they exist, regardless of how much the person concerned pleads with them and denies that they wrote them. The mental health team will be especially well covered by the Mental Health Act if they make the claim at the same time that it is within that person's interest. I have known this to happen. When a patient complained that a social worker had started the procedure to have them certified, using this as evidence, her complaint about it was not upheld. They wrote and told her that to look at the alleged letters would be in breach of confidentiality to her, the patient. The mind boggles. Maybe it was more a case of the social worker being incompetent, and they were grasping at straws.

Although I have stated that health officials are the only profession where it's virtually impossible to get anything done about a complaint, I do remember the days when it was bad, maybe even worse, in the church. Yet at least you could complain about it without endangering yourself; a vicar has no power over his congregation and people aren't frightened of him. During the early 1950s I can remember hearing my parents talking about a vicar who was permanently drunk, doing one mad thing after another. These days he could readily be dismissed.

It's the same in the Post Office. If a postman is clearly drunk, he has to go. I know you do get cases where they aren't delivering the letters but letting them mount up inside their own home. One postman dumped the lot in the river, but after this was discovered he was no longer a postman.

I have also heard a couple of times of something similar happening with the newspapers. A reporter was supposed to be asking the passengers on a train their opinion on public transport, and instead he simply sat at home and made it all up. In a similar case a court reporter found it simpler to go inside the public house and write up the cases over a drink. The editor sweated when he realised what had happened and wondered what legal action he was open to. His mind was put to rest when he discovered that every name and address was fictional, and he was even more relieved when no questions were asked and no one seemed to realise this. Some people would say, "Obviously he had to go" but I know that may not be the case. I have had shock after shock, not so much at what some people can get away with but what damage it can do.

I haven't heard yet of a member of the Mental Health Team

drinking, but as regards everything else I know about there's no way round it that's simple and straightforward. If anything comes under criminal law then forget it, the police will soon fob you off – uniforms stick together. I have already mentioned the Human Rights Act but the patient may not find out about it in enough time and the Mental Health Act remains the main body of legislation. Suing them for anything else they may be in breach of is traumatising. It can come too late and you may lose all your money. You might be fast winning, but then you run out of funds so the case is never finished. The staff belong to strong unions which have substantial funds, and they would soon be able to find an astute lawyer who would defend the case successfully, and if he was not scrupulous he might even make certain that you would lose all your money.

But on a different note, and back to the Middle Ages. Most extraordinarily of all they would blame a child for being illegitimate, entirely against nature and common sense. I remember in my childhood when little black or mixed-race babies started appearing out of wedlock and my elders were saying, "Really, those American soldiers are the absolute limit!" They didn't blame the child. It would still be a dear little baby. It does make me wonder if it is only the sad cases we hear about from days gone by. We don't know about the ones which are not discovered. Even these days, with birth certificates and adoption papers, we still don't have to tell everyone all our business. Maybe in the past many more illegitimate babies were accepted and loved than we realise; maybe they were swapped and moved around more than we know. Or are so many of us so just indoctrinated? I know fear can do so much

Chapter One

STAIRWAY TO THE PAST

Jessica and Peggy Newton were fifteen years old when they moved to Bowdon in 1959. Their mother had died two years previously. Their father was failing in business and was in deep trouble for fiddling the books; he had been charged with fraud, was pleading guilty and might well face prison. But Jessica and Peggy, who were non-identical twins, knew none of this. They only knew that their father could not afford to keep them in London any longer.

They were staying with their grandmother in a big house in Stamford Road, with a big garden and a high wooden fence and gate. The house had plenty of rooms and old Mrs Newton waited on them hand and foot. She hoped they would never find out about their father, and what had happened with his business.

The girls loved living in Bowdon, having frequently been there before during school holidays. They loved the long bicycle rides they could go on, which would take them so quickly into the country. Yet the area nearby was fun too. They would race faster and faster along South Downs Road, finding it all very exciting, squealing round the corners and overtaking one another with their hands behind their backs.

One day Jessica was riding in Hale when a middle-aged man drew up alongside her on his motorbike and said "You are an absolute menace on the roads!" There was a woman riding pillion behind him, scowling furiously at Jessica and nodding in agreement with everything he said. It wouldn't have bothered Jessica, but he finished up by saying, "And I don't know what your folk are thinking of to allow you to have a bicycle."

In fact they didn't allow it; they had forbidden it. An earlier incident like this had got back to her grandmother shortly before, and she wondered who had told her. She wondered if it was the woman who was always looking out of the window of the big old house on South Downs Road. Peggy also wondered what had made her look up, as she was always so busy racing round the corner. One day she had even gone back on foot with Jessica and gone inside the garden, yet all she could see was a figure, and Jessica said she could see no one. They had dashed away when someone came to the door.

But for now Mrs Newton had spoken to their father about it. He said "Lock their bicycles up in the shed until they are 21". She had done so, but the girls had got them out again. They hid them behind a hedge at the bottom of the garden, knowing they could get out the back way on to Winton Road. Their grandmother didn't notice, but it still bothered Jessica. What would happen if this man on the motor bike ever came face to face with one of their folk and told them about it?

Then they had another scare. One day they were out sharing a bicycle, going down Vicarage Lane into Bowdon Vale, Jessica riding and Peggy on the handlebars, when suddenly she noticed that a police car was waiting for them at the bottom of the hill.

"Stop, stop!" called out Peggy. "It's the police waiting for us." Jessica merely called back "I'm trying to stop, but the brakes won't work." They literally rode straight into the arms of the law. A police officer asked for their address, and they gave the address of someone they didn't like. It made them nervous when he said he was going round to their house to see their parents about it.

They felt especially afraid when a few days later they saw the same police officer walking across the road in the direction of their house. They could see him because a gale had blown down their wooden fence, but they gave out a sigh of relief when he went straight by.

Mrs Newton was sitting quietly by the window and had pushed a table up to it so that she could eat her dinner and look out at the same time. She merely got on with her meal. She had no idea how near they had been to an explosion. But she found out anyway, because the girls were frequently out and about on their bikes. Someone had said to her, "I often see the girls riding in Hale, they're so fearless." She wondered what she should do about it. It was very inconvenient for them not to have their bikes, so she and their father decided to talk to them about it. They imposed strict conditions for being allowed to have them back.

This didn't stop them from tearing down South Downs Road again, and they decided to try once again to see who the woman was who was always looking out of the window. This did slow them down. Nervously they walked up the path. A stout middle-aged woman arrived at the front door; they later found out that she was called Mrs Lomax. She looked more like the daily help, and a rough one at that, wearing a very old-fashioned apron, although in fact it was her house and she lived there on her own.

She began to demand to know who they were. They mumbled that they were wondering who had been looking out of the window but dashed away when they stared. She snapped that she lived on her own. "There's no one up there at all!" she said.

The girls frequently went for walks as well as rides. They would go along Green Walk and on to the Devisdale, which was just fields and no houses at that time, although there was talk of building. It was full of people taking their dogs out for a walk.

One day they came across a tree which looked like a weeping willow. It had branches that hung down low and leaves so thick they had to touch them to make certain they weren't cloth. It was covered in colourful flowers, and very beautiful.

Under the tree they were surprised to find a little wooden house. It was almost small and colourful enough to be a doll's house. But as they went up the path towards the house, they were surprised by the amount of space that opened up around them. It was as though it was expanding as they walked.

They went inside the house and decided to call it Willow Tree Cottage. It seemed very old-fashioned. They saw some shabby old clothes lying on the floor, which appeared to date back hundreds of years. They must have belonged to someone very poor. In the middle of the room was a fireplace.

"Let's light it!" said Jessica.

"Are you trying to set the place alight?" replied Peggy.

Yet it did look as though a fire had been burning there recently. It took them back some years, and made them want to play house.

Then, just when they were about to settle down, they looked through the window to see a man coming towards them. They wondered how they could escape. They weren't supposed to be there.

They quickly ducked down and realised that they couldn't run into the next room, as there wasn't one. They slowly got up to peep out of the window to find that the man was still approaching. They were surprised at how clearly they could see him through the branches; in fact, there didn't seem to be so many branches any more. They had both climbed trees in the past and knew how clearly you can see from them, and how the people below can't see you, so maybe it was the same if you are inside a tree house.

They ducked down again. The third time they peeped out of the window the man had gone right past. "I wonder if he saw us?" said Jessica.

They met the man next day in Bowdon Post Office at the top of Richmond Road, buying some stamps. He worked for the council, the council offices being next door but one to the post office, in a house called Scrivien House. They mentioned to him where they had seen him before, but told a lie. They said they'd been standing outside Willow Tree Cottage instead of inside it.

"What cottage?" he laughed. "Who do you think you're kidding?" He turned round to someone else in the queue and said, still grinning all over his face, "I reckon it's her next door that's started all this off, she's mad enough."

Jessica and Peggy didn't know what to say. He went on to tell them, "If you think you're fooling me, you're not." He still looked amused.

"How do you mean?" asked Peggy.

"With all these ideas that there's a cottage there."

"But there is!"

Everyone in the post office turned round and laughed.

"So you found it and went inside?" said the man from the council.

"Yes."

"And you walked past while we were in it" said Jessica.

Another customer who clearly thought it was all a joke said, "You're not the only one that's heard this rumour."

"No one has said anything to us about it, the first we knew of it was when we saw it."

"But it's never been proved that it's there. In fact it has been proved that it isn't."

"It's in a tree."

"In a tree!" exclaimed the postmistress. Everyone chuckled with laughter and one person said, "I've heard that one before. Every tree on the Devisdale has been looked into."

"It gets bigger as you go up the path, or at least the garden does" said Peggy, but this was met by more laughter.

The assumption was being made that the woman next door had started some kind of hysteria, simply because she did sometimes do strange things. She had some paranoid notices on her window, though there was no mention on them of Willow Tree Cottage. The twins left the post office and went home together. They felt hungry and were ready for tea.

They got up early next morning and went straight to see the little house. They found it much as before. Inside it was much the same too, except that there was now a mirror lying on the floor.

Peggy picked it up. She looked into it – and let out a shriek. It was not her face she had seen in it, but another; the face of a young girl of about her own age.

"Peggy!" said the girl in the mirror, yearningly, "Please get me out of here!"

"Get you out of where?" Peggy couldn't believe what she was seeing. The girl was small with longish fair hair and she was wearing a long blue dress.

"I died in the plague in 1665," she said.

"But the plague was in London!"

"It spread to other places."

"Did it come to Bowdon?"

"Well I'm buried in Bowdon Churchyard."

"What's your name?"

"Catherine Sellars"

"I'll do my best for you Catherine" said Peggy, and put the mirror down.

"What's that?" asked Jessica, who had only heard bits of this bizarre conversation. She did know her sister had shown signs before of having some strange gifts.

"Let's go, and I'll tell you" she replied, and they headed off home together.

As everyone else had laughed at their story of the cottage, they expected their grandmother to do the same, so they told her nothing. But they did go into Bowdon Church to check up on the parish records. They found that a Catherine Sellars, aged 15, had died of the plague in the 17th century and been buried there. It was Canon Lowe who showed it them.

"What, in Bowdon?" they both exclaimed. They couldn't understand it.

"Records can be wrong" he said. "There can be corruption, we will never know. The people who could tell us have long gone."

They both knew that the plague had spread like wildfire and that if someone caught it they were dead in no time.

They talked on. "She couldn't have travelled up from London with that! She'd have died on the way," said Peggy. "Maybe someone else gave it her who had just come up from there, but wouldn't they too be dead on arrival?"

"Maybe they quickly buried her to get it hushed up and to stop it spreading" said Canon Lowe. He told them how it had struck Stockport in 1605 and spread to other places, yet they still found it difficult to accept.

"They say it was the fleas on black rats that did it. Maybe it was just one rat that travelled in a wagon, many of them have travelled much further on boats" said Jessica.

"It can travel in cloth."

"That's more likely."

* * * *

Next morning they had to start their new school. The summer holidays were over and they still couldn't go back to London. Their grandmother wondered if she should tell them how bad things were, that it was getting more likely that their father would go to prison, and in any case, there were other problems. But she decided to say nothing. The girls had enough to think about.

"It's only for a few months" said Jessica. "I'll be 16 next year, and then I'll be able to get a job in Woolworths."

"You will not!" said their grandmother. "You'll go on to learn office skills or something like that."

"I won't!"

Neither of the girls was clever. They went to a little private girls' school called Broussa High in Broomfield Lane, later to become Hale Preparatory School, near Hale Railway Station. They were the new girls, and they were far from made welcome. One of them, Sarah, clearly intended getting up a crowd against them.

"Keep away from them, they smell!" she jeered, holding her nose. Jessica rushed to pick up a chair and held it high above her saying, "What's that you've just said about me?" She tried to bring it down on to Sarah's head, but the other girl kept ducking. Her cronies came forward to help her, but Peggy stood in the way to stop them and a struggle broke out. When it seemed that the twins were losing because there were too many of them, Peggy managed to pick up a vase and hit one of them on the head with it.

It was a wonder the vase didn't break. The girl staggered about as though she was going to faint, clearly going dizzy, but she didn't want to admit defeat. Sarah continued to back away from Jessica, who kept the chair up high and continued to ask her "What's that you said about us?" At times they appeared paralysed, all of them, except Jessica and Peggy, almost as though a spell had been put on them, but then Peggy did have some strange powers.

Sarah started walking towards the door, trying to make it look as though she was casually walking out, but Jessica got there first and stood in the way. Holding the chair down just a little, she asked her again, "What was it you just said?"

Jessica looked at the vase and wondered if she should use that instead, but another girl tried to grab it and take it away. Peggy stopped her. "We want that" she said. Another girl rushed forward and tried to grab it off her saying "you're mad!" and a free fight broke out. The whole lot of them, complete with the vase, fell down into a heap on the floor with Jessica and Peggy at the bottom.

Just then the door opened to reveal a teacher standing there. She made the assumption that some of the girls were picking on a new girl and so, half gently to Jessica and Peggy and half speaking sharply to the rest of them, she told them to stop it. "The bell will soon be going" she said. After this nothing more was said about it, and as time went by they even became friends with Sarah.

That afternoon, instead of going straight home after school, Jessica and Peggy went back to Willow Tree Cottage. They found everything exactly the same: the mirror, the chair, the fireplace. Peggy picked up the mirror and looked into it to see Catherine again. This time her hand came out and grasped Peggy's wrist. "Oh Peggy, get me out of here!" she pleaded.

"I'm doing my best."

"I know you are. Something keeps telling me it won't be long now."

Peggy was pleased about that. She was beginning to realise that she had strange powers. This was getting through to Catherine, yet she didn't know how this girl was doing it.

"Catherine" said Peggy, "If you yearn and yearn, and plead and plead, and if I try and try, then I think you could be out soon."

They had to go, and started on their way home again. They stopped at Brookes, the grocer shop on the corner of Stamford and Richmond Road. Mrs Newton had asked them to do a bit of shopping for her. It was difficult to get served, as all the staff were making up orders, but when they eventually did, they asked if any of them knew about the tree house on the Devisdale. They got treated more seriously here, and one woman said, "No, I don't know, but I would like to." She said she had seen it, and heard singing coming from it. That was interesting, but the girls had to go on their way.

When they got to the gate they found Catherine standing there.

"Thank you, thank you for getting me out" she said.

They invited her in, and told their grandmother that Catherine was a friend from school. They explained her clothing by saying she had been in a school play and that she was still in fancy dress. They all sat round and had tea together. It amused them that Catherine sounded the 'k' as well as 'n' when using the word 'knife', making it into two syllables.

"That's real old-fashioned English" said Mrs Newton. "But they pronounce the k as well in Esperanto, and that's a man-made language."

After tea they went upstairs to find Catherine something different to wear, something up to date. She found it all very strange. "I can't wear that!" she exclaimed when trying on a dress. When she looked in the mirror she laughed. It looked comical to her, yet it looked like an ordinary dress to Jessica and Peggy.

"What's wrong with it?" they asked.

"People can see my legs!"

"Only a little bit, and in any case, we'll give you long socks to wear with it."

But Catherine still didn't like it. They didn't like to tell her that a new fashion was coming called the new line, and skirts would go up to just below the knee. None of them knew that they were going to get very much shorter still in the decades to come and that it would no longer be possible to wear suspenders any more, so they would all have to wear tights. But for now they got on with trying on clothes with Catherine.

She next tried on a very full skirt with a net petticoat underneath it, which made it stick out. She liked it. "Isn't it old fashioned?" she said. It reminded her of the Elizabethan style.

"Grandma says it's possible to be so old fashioned that you can call yourself ahead of the fashion" said Peggy. "Styles come round again."

She wouldn't be able to ride a bicycle with that" said Jessica, and brought out a pair of trousers. Catherine thought they were hilarious.

"Only men wear trousers and I've never seen a pair like that in any case" she laughed.

"Women can wear them too" said Peggy.

"Only a few" put in Jessica.

In fact there had recently been a letter in the newspapers about it. Four girls had gone for a day out by the seaside, all four of them in trousers, but they kept getting disapproving looks, so they wrote to the papers saying they were free to wear what they liked. They wondered what was wrong with everyone and signed themselves "four disgusted girls."

Eventually the twins persuaded Catherine to have a full, grey skirt, a pink jumper with a high neck and a pair of long socks. They told her that she would be drawing attention to herself if she went about in the dress she'd arrived in, and she did very much like the pink jumper. She also liked the pair of old ballet shoes they gave her.

They came downstairs and asked their grandmother if Catherine could stay the night. "Most certainly not!" was the reply, so they put her on a camp bed in the outside shed.

Later on their grandmother remarked "I feel awful not having her. Clearly she's undernourished and not being looked after properly, but I can't."

"Well at least she's not got the plague" said Peggy.

Mrs Newton laughed, but Peggy had a point.

The next morning, they got up very early and crept out of the house before their grandmother woke up. The three of them were going to the Devisdale and taking the camp bed and some blankets with them for Catherine. They hung about for a short while, which made them very late for school. When they arrived a teacher was marching towards them.

"You can't do this here!" she bawled. She was followed by another teacher walking close behind, who was also shouting at them never to dare to be so late again. They were late again the next day but managed to get in without being seen. They were always on time after that.

During the week Catherine continued to visit them, but she was homesick and desperately wanted to go back in time, to be with her mother. Peggy seized the opportunity to ask her, "How did you manage to die of the plague in Bowdon?"

"Oh, the infection travelled in all sorts of things, and I was pushed about all over the place. My mother had worked for some very rich people and was able to get me out. In fact, it was suspected that I was the daughter of a rich man she'd been with, maybe even royalty."

At Willow Tree Cottage they had noticed that in one corner of the room there was a door. The next time they visited, they opened it, expecting to find a cupboard. They had a surprise when they saw what was behind it. Instead of a cupboard it concealed a steep flight of stone steps, which appeared to go down into some sort of a cellar.

"Come on, let's see what's down there" said Jessica. Carefully they climbed down into the darkness, and Catherine started getting very excited. "I'm going back home, I'm going back home!" she kept saying as they went down and down into the blackness.

Peggy and Jessica noticed that as they went down, all their clothes were gradually changing. It was not long before they all appeared to be dressed as if for the early 17th century. Finally they came to a door, and opened it to find themselves looking into bright sunshine and a very busy street. A horse and carriage went past. They had gone back nearly 300 years in time.

Catherine now found herself feeling very much at home. In fact it was she who was now the confident one, the one who walked ahead while the twins followed nervously behind. This wasn't for long, for they soon caught up with her and began to walk by her side.

Despite the stench they rather liked the narrow streets filled with people and the wooden-framed houses, built high and leaning towards one another. The houses were so close that the girls could see two women in upstairs windows facing each other, having a quiet talk together. If they'd been any nearer they could have reached across and shaken hands.

She thought some of the women in the street looked hideous the way they had made their faces up. It was a ghastly white colour, because the make-up came from poisonous lead, and if they smiled it cracked. It also smelled foul. On top of this people were using bits of mouse skin to make their eyebrows look stylish. Yet Catherine didn't seem to mind, in fact she made no mention of it. Maybe it was a fashion she was well used to. They wondered what she thought about the make-up of the 1950s. Would she think mascara was hideous?

There was a beggar crawling along the ground, obviously desperate. With pitiful eyes he looked up at a man who was clearly very rich. "Do you have any money?" the beggar asked.

"Yes, lots of it" the man sternly replied, and went on his way without giving him a farthing.

"I think that's dreadful!" said Jessica to Catherine, who agreed with her. Then Peggy said, "They say that if drugs start becoming a problem we'll have lots of begging coming back on to our streets. It'll be a common thing to see even in the 1960s and 70s."

"Who said that?" asked Jessica, for it was the first she'd heard of it, in fact it was the first she'd heard of drugs being a problem. Peggy had vaguely heard something about it when she had been in a newsagent's shop, a place she'd go to early every morning to deliver newspapers. She had asked the newsagent what it was all about and he explained a little to her.

"I wouldn't have to pay you any more if I could get you addicted to that stuff" he said. "In fact I wouldn't need to get you to give out newspapers any more. I could get a lot more by putting you out on the streets as a prostitute. You'd work for me and I could take all the money."

She was horrified that he could suggest such a thing. She told her father he had said it, expecting him to be very shocked, but he just said, "Yes that's right. If a man can get you addicted to drugs, you'll be his slave."

She had no time to think about this now as they walked on along the narrow streets, passing the rich and the poor. They found that people were highly suspicious of one another. One man pointed at another, and then, looking straight at the girls, he said, "Never trust a man who wears a French hat." Yet it was the Dutch who they really didn't trust, as England had had so many wars with them. Catherine especially didn't trust them. She said they had been coming in along the River Thames.

"But I thought all the fighting was about fishing somewhere miles away in America and the enemy couldn't get across to us because of the sea?" said Jessica.

"Which war are you talking about?" asked Catherine. "We've had so many with the Dutch."

She knew that they had indeed got across the sea to the River Thames, but the English had soon seen them off. She also told them about another battle she'd heard about first hand, the battle of Lowestoft. The Dutch were defeated. Everyone in London went by the riverside and into the park to hear the guns going off to celebrate it.

Peggy and Jessica were both thoughtful. They knew their father had been shooting the planes down when the Germans were bombing London, and they knew what a hazard the River Thames had been. It meant they could use it as a landmark, to find their way about. If it wasn't for the Thames they might not have been able to find London at all. When they said so to Catherine, she asked what a plane was.

"Oh we've shown you one" they said. "We're near an airport"

"Yes, but you didn't tell me they were used for that, to drop bombs on people. It frightens me. Don't worry me with the future, the present is bad enough with all this fighting. If it's going to get worse I want to stay in the 17th Century."

They were just recovering from the Civil War between Parliament and King Charles I. His son Charles II had been restored to the throne, but old rivalries still remained and there was still tension between the Protestants and the Catholics there.

They walked on. Dead dogs were rotting on the street. They

overhead a man saying that there had been the body of a man floating on the river Thames for three days, that it was barbaric, and time they cleared it up. Catherine continued to lead the way. There were no road signs, yet she was in no way lost. People would go by the shops. A dragon mark meant a chemist and an Adam and Eve sign meant a fruit shop.

They went into one of them. It smelt exotic, scented with a myriad herbs, dried mint, aniseed, clovers and ginger. It was a place of wonder, sparkling array of colourful bottles and jars tightly corked. Dried herbs hung from the ceiling and baskets and boxes of sandalwood were piled on every counter. They didn't want to leave it, but they had no money so they had to go.

Then they went past a place that looked like a hospital.

"Would you like to be a nurse?" Jessica asked Catherine.

"What do you mean?" she exclaimed. She realised they didn't know what a nurse was, not in 1665.

"Well, would you like to look after the sick?" Peggy asked her. "No thanks!" she replied.

They continued to have a very confused conversation about hospitals. It seemed to be the first time Catherine had heard that they were places for the sick; she considered them as places for hospitality, to give people shelter. She thought of them as somewhere appalling, places that were staffed by drunks, convicts, anyone, in return for shelter themselves. No wonder she'd sounded insulted at being asked if she'd like to be a nurse. It seemed that they too were regarded as something appalling.

"Well what about curing the sick?" asked Peggy.

"Yes. They use leeches to suck their blood, but not in a hospital, they do it in the home."

"Is that all they do?"

"No, they cut out stones from the kidneys."

"How painful!"

"Some of these operations are not as bad as they sound. They make people very drunk, then they get heavy labourers to hold them down."

"What else do they do?"

"How do I know? Do you know everything about curing the sick in 1959?"

"No."

The girls noticed that Catherine seemed to think that cure of the body and care of the soul were very closely linked.

It was very hot and dry, yet the girls noticed that some of the people were using fire. It was needed to cook on; one house was burning coal and another wood. They wondered where they were going, and asked Catherine, who told them they were going to see Ginger, her boyfriend.

They soon found him. He worked for a baker called Thomas Farryner in Pudding Lane. They couldn't see why he was called Ginger, as his hair was hardly ginger, just a little sandy. He was just finishing up cleaning up an oven and was pleased to see Catherine. She went into the back of the shop to talk to Ginger while the twins stayed in the front with a woman who worked for them called Bessie, who lived upstairs.

When Catherine came out of the back of the shop she said she had to go and see her mother.

"Hang on a minute, I'll come with you" said Ginger, coming out just behind her. They didn't really want him. How would they explain where they were going afterwards – back to the staircase, back to the Devisdale and into the future, 1959? He might want to come with them, and how would they manage that?

Yet Catherine was so pleased to have him walking by her side as they chatted away. The girls wondered how they could ignore such things as ashes and dust being constantly thrown out on to the street and piles of dung lying about everywhere. Ginger noticed their disgust.

"Where do you come from, the country?" he asked them. "This is nothing, we've had central London flooded out, the river Thames has been frozen over for several winters and at low tide it stinks. At the best of times it's full of floating corpses."

"When we were coming here there was a man saying it was barbaric to have a body left in the water for three days."

"Where's he come from, Fantasy Island? We've got them all the time."

Then an old woman came out of her house, very distressed. "Oh I daren't face my next door neighbour with this again!" she cried, "He's been so patient with me when it's happened before."

"What's that?" asked Ginger and Catherine. It turned out that the cesspit from her cellar had flooded next door. They followed her down into it to have a look.

"Any chance we can get in next door?" asked Ginger.

"Plenty, and he's out at the moment" she told them. The four of them followed her into it and began to work. It was a really mucky job, but with four of them on it, it was soon getting done.

Then Jessica started saying they had to get back, as their grandmother would be wondering where they were.

"You go, I'll finish off" said Ginger.

They were glad of an excuse not to have him with them any more. As they went along Catherine explained how very like him it all was. He was always willing to oblige and didn't ask questions.

As they walked through the streets, the girls said, "We must get back, Grandma will be wondering where we are."

"She won't. Time stands still while we are here" said Catherine.

"Really, does it?"

This seemed unlikely, as it was beginning to get dark. They could see that inside the houses people were lighting coal and log fires and had candles burning. They walked on until they were outside the city wall. Finally they came to a big house and a woman came running out.

"Catherine, what are you doing here?" she said. It was her mother. Clearly she was pleased to see her daughter, although she went on to say that she shouldn't be there. She was a governess in the house and she invited them in. The place was full of workmen.

"Oh he's like this all the time" she told them, talking about the man she worked for, the owner of the house. "He's always decorating and improving the place." At this particular time they were rebuilding the staircase and enlarging a window, but shortly before he had put in an extra storey and a new chimney pot and had smartened up the cellar. He was keen on a display of pictures, built-in bookshelves and a room for entertaining. Yet at the same time, like all houses of the time, there was the smell of unwashed bodies and dirty hair, and the chamber pots that had to be carried up and down the stairs. They would sometimes even spill over a little

But her mother was there to teach the children. She had to go. She and Catherine hugged each other and then they went their separate ways.

* * * * *

Catherine continued to lead the way through the streets.

"Were you born in that house?" asked Peggy.

"I don't know. I just get told not to ask too many questions."

As they walked on, Catherine volunteered a little more. "If you want to know the honest truth, they think I may be the illegitimate child of someone quite high up in the government. Some of my childhood I had to spend sleeping on the streets because I had to be hidden away, and sometimes I would go up to this big house and be with my mother and treated as royalty."

A horse and carriage came along. It came very close to them and they had to squeeze up next to the wall to let it go past, yet no one else seemed to feel afraid of being trampled on. They came to the door through which they had arrived and went back up the steps to find they were back in the house on the Devisdale. No one knew where they'd been. But they found that Catherine was right; time had stood still, it was the same time as when they had left.

Chapter Two

CATHERINE AND GINGER

It was up first thing in the morning for the girls, and off to school. There was just one thing to do before they went, which was to go into the garage with two pieces of toast and a cup of tea for Catherine; she had spent the night there. Another camp bed had been found for her.

"You know, that was a big risk I took, going back to London" she told them. "I could have got the plague."

They asked her what she intended doing that day. She told them she'd be all right; she'd spend it in Willow Tree Cottage.

"But it's so boring!"

"I'll be OK."

They noticed that she had put her long blue dress back on, as she didn't feel comfortable in the other. "A long dress these days looks barmy" said Peggy. "You'll be laughed and jeered at and called a crank if you wear that."

"But I did what you said and shortened it."

She stood up. The dress no longer went down to the ground. In fact, although still quite long, it was now a reasonable length for 1959.

The girls picked up the sewing basket and put it back in the house before their grandmother could miss it; she had taken it out of the front room. They didn't mention to Catherine that she had sewn it up very badly and that you could see some very big stitches in it, and the hem was crooked.

As they cycled off down Stamford Road, Catherine was walking up it. Two girls from her school overtook them on their bicycles, sounding their bells loudly as they did so. "Who's that old tramp you're with?" they shouted.

"Don't know what you're talking about" they shouted back, yet it did worry them that Catherine looked so scruffy and was attracting attention to herself.

Next they heard a wolf whistle. It was a young lad racing past on his bicycle from Altrincham Boys' Grammar School; it was Catherine he was whistling at.

"That's not a tramp!" shouted Peggy at him.

"Best looking girl in Bowdon!" he shouted back.

Just before the morning break they had a singing lesson. The teacher banged away at the piano as they all sang away "London's burning, London's burning", Jessica and Peggy especially singing with enthusiasm. It would take them a long time to forget the day before. They remembered some of the things they'd seen in old London, for example the candles burning. Why didn't they use lanterns, as Guy Fawkes had when there was gunpowder about? They remembered how she had seen the baker cleaning out the oven and not doing it very well. That can start a fire.

Then the bell went, time for break. They all poured out into the playground. Two of the girls hid behind a bush to smoke.

"Make sure you don't set that on fire" they said to her.

"Oh, shurrup!"

"No we won't."

Then a teacher came along. She soon shifted them, saying she would tell their parents. Next they saw Catherine looking over the hedge from Broomfield Lane and went to talk to her.

The bell went, time to go back for lessons. Old Mrs Taylor from next door came out of her big house and invited Catherine in. Mrs Taylor was ancient, and she walked with a terrible stoop and very slowly. One girl made a joke of it. She said, "She's dead modern she is, she's doing the creep." The creep was a dance that was still popular at the time, but not everyone thought it was a good joke, particularly the parents who had heard it.

However, Mrs Taylor knew nothing of this and said she'd give Catherine a bite to eat. Catherine accepted the invitation. Clearly she looked deprived. A teacher asked Jessica who she was.

"I don't know, she just looked needy, so I went to speak to her."

"That was very kind of you."

Things went on much the same for the next week or two, but they made the history teacher very happy by asking her about the history of nursing. She didn't enquire as to why they had developed this sudden interest, but she told them how everything had been in a mess until Florence Nightingale came along. In fact nursing couldn't really be called nursing before that, as the interest of the "nurses" was to get money, regardless of how unscrupulous it all was. Drink and theft were common problems, even sometimes prostitution.

In 1834 in Britain, all that began to change. France and Britain had declared war on Russia and for two years they fought the Crimean War. The loss of life was colossal, but those who died did so not so much from wounds but from the diseases that followed, brought about by dreadful living conditions. It was much published in the newspapers that the "hospitals" of the time were poorly staffed, with insufficient supplies, and the sanitary and medical conditions were awful.

Florence Nightingale travelled across with 38 other voluntary nurses to relieve the situation. They did this with much success and although she only stayed a couple of years before returning back home and spent the rest of her life as an invalid herself, she nevertheless continued to do much to promote nursing, changing it forever. This was how *The Times* described her:

She is a ministering angel without any exaggeration in these hospitals, and as her slender form glides quietly along each corridor, every poor fellow's face softens with gratitude at the sight of her. When all the medical officers have retired for the night and silence and darkness has settled down upon those miles of prostrate sick, she may be observed alone, with a little lamp in her hand, doing her solitary rounds.

* * * * *

Things continued to run smoothly along, even though the post office was having a very trying time with the woman next door, Mrs Ravenscroft, nicknamed Queenie. She was getting a lot worse with her shouting and ranting at them, saying that she had a photograph of everyone who went in there and also that everything they said was tape recorded. In those days a tape recorder would be something as big as a suitcase that you would have to carry around with you and of course no one believed her. A lot of people said she wouldn't even know how to take a photograph, and yet at the same time they would cross the road when approaching the house.

One reason for this was that Mrs Ravenscroft was very fond of throwing a bucket of water over them and would keep one permanently waiting for them behind her front door. She seemed to have perfect faith that it would be an ideal defence. Every now and again there would be a big blow-up about it; for example once she threw one over the postman when he came to empty the letter box.

She would write the neighbours crazy letters, especially to young girls, and it was obvious she was jealous. She would put her full name and address on them, so clearly she didn't think she was doing anything wrong. She would accuse them of calling her a tart and then go on to say that they were tarts. It was as though she was having a nightmare; it was all things people couldn't say they wouldn't dream of, especially the women, and some of it would be most Freudian. It would be written on paper roughly torn out of an exercise book, and obviously done in a terrible rage because of the jagged edges. It would also be full of blots and appalling spelling, and yet it was strange; on top of all this you could tell she was an educated lady.

Mrs Ravenscroft was continually having her windows broken by yobs. They would both be enjoying having a good old slanging match, so much so that the house became known as "The House with Broken Windows". Again mad notices would be put on them saying things like "Broken by the Holy Hypocrites". A lot of people didn't realise that she meant by this that people coming home from church were doing it, and again her spelling would be completely haywire. It was also suspected at times that she had broken the windows herself in order to get her point across. At least once this was easily provable, yet on other occasions it was provable that she hadn't.

Eventually they did come and section her, but not many people realised that the real reason for this was that they were progressing in medication and thought they might be able to do something for her. No one could understand why they kept her in for so long, but it would simply be that some of these drugs can take some time to work. In fact some people who had previously said "She needs putting away" started saying instead "They should let her out", especially when they heard that she had behaved herself ever since she'd been in there. Maybe they didn't feel safe themselves, if you could get nine months for causing an obstruction in a shop doorway.

However the hospital failed dismally; Mrs Ravenscroft remained as mad as a hatter forever after. And yet it seemed they had cured her of one thing. It no longer worried her that she was mad, for they didn't tell her she wasn't. Instead they showed her, by putting her on a ward with people who were worse, much worse. She telephoned one of the neighbours while she was in there and said "Oh I've got some stories to tell you when I come out, it's <u>mad</u> in here!" Before then she had clearly had a complex about it, going round accusing everyone else of being mad, even if they were quite stable, but now all of that had stopped.

* * * * *

Catherine spent a lot of time at Jessica's and Peggy's rather than at Willow Tree Cottage. She found it all such a novelty, and Mrs Newton found it fascinating that she was so curious. She even found her once lying on the floor trying to look up the chimney.

"Is getting rid of all the smoke really as simple as that?" she asked.

"It most certainly isn't" replied Mrs Newton, telling her how in history they'd had trouble for years where a chimney had caught fire, too much soot accumulating, and that solving it by getting them cleaned out had created another problem. 'Climbing boys', as chimney sweeps were called, had horrific accidents. One man who campaigned for it to be stopped had lived just a few doors away in Stamford Road, Bowdon. His name was William Wood and he was buried in Bowdon Church.

"So it's all sorted out now?"

"Yes, and in any case they're bringing in central heating. In fact some people have already got it."

"That's a shame, I like a log or coal fire" said Catherine.

"It's all very old fashioned" said Peggy "The Romans had it."

"Stop being so daft."

"Well they did, the Romans did have central heating."

"I still say it's not old fashioned."

As regards Bowdon Church, Catherine had been up there with Jessica and Peggy to a youth club, but she only dared show her head round the door. A lot of the other girls there were nursery nurses from Ingledene, a children's home in Richmond Road. She marvelled at how Protestants and Catholics mixed together without fighting. She made mention of this to Mrs Newton.

"Well, we're in it now for the right reason aren't we, not just for power" she said. She did tell her that a Roman Catholic isn't allowed to go into an Anglican church without getting special permission from the priest first, for things like weddings and funerals.

"They say they're going to stop all that" said Peggy.

Another time Catherine exclaimed "Look at that! What sort of a carriage is that and how can it get into the sky?" She could never get used to planes.

Mrs Newton laughed. She now felt certain that some of the time Catherine was taking the mickey. "I do agree that plane is very low" she said. "You can even see what's written on the door, in fact I've never seen one as low as that before even though we live so near to the airport."

"Well I've seen plenty in Stockport" said Peggy. "It's like a bus that goes up in the sky."

Jessica started keeping a diary of everything that happened. "He rode his bicycle close to mine, I wonder if he fancies me" she wrote. It was Philip Lane from Altrincham Boys' School she was talking about. She found out he did fancy her when he came round to see her that evening. Mrs Newton didn't like it; she said it was too late.

"It's not night, you can't call six o'clock night" Jessica insisted.

"Well it's dark, so I do" she protested. But their father phoned them up that evening and agreed with his daughters that it wasn't.

"It's still too late" said Mrs Newton.

"It's not night until eight o'clock, and in any case, they'll be 16 next year and we'll have to let them out then until eleven" he replied.

Mrs Newton nearly fainted. She preferred a quiet night in with the girls safely indoors. Consequently she decided to encourage Catherine to come to the house more often; she was happy just to sit in the back kitchen and have a quiet cup of coffee. She didn't seem to have any family that took an interest. Mrs Newton couldn't get a straight answer if she asked.

Philip Lane continued to ride his bicycle near to Jessica's, overtaking her each morning on his way to school. This gave her more to write about in her diary, and more still when she arrived at school. She found she had rivalry. She was thrilled when she discovered that someone else wanted him and that it was making her jealous. She especially liked it that he seemed to be choosing her instead. It made it better still that she had an audience.

"He's mine" another girl told her in front of everyone, and they all laughed. Shortly after that he got tired of them both and would frequently be seen riding alongside a girl from Culcheth Hall, another private girls' school nearby, on the corner of Cavendish Road and Ashley Road and later to become Bowdon Preparatory School.

Jessica had ridden a motorbike, although she had never properly got the hang of it. She'd known a young lad who'd had one and let her have a go sometimes, and she loved to go out with him and ride pillion.

One evening at about five o'clock they heard the roar of a bike outside their gate. It was another young lad come to see Jessica. She was surprised, as she didn't know him all that well. She didn't even know he knew where she lived.

He had come to take her out on the bike. They went down to the River Bollin together and she had another go at riding. She discovered she wasn't as bad as she thought she was, and in fact she was a fast learner. The lad's name was Peter Brown and she went out with him on the back of his bike quite a few times after that. Sometimes they would go to see someone they knew who lived in Bowgreen Road, and she would practise riding it on her own up and down there.

While the girls would talk endlessly about boys, Catherine would talk endlessly about Ginger, saying she had to go to see him as he might otherwise emigrate. During the 17th century more and more people were going to North America, and she had heard terrible things about it. Some of them didn't even survive the journey. They would die of such things as sea sickness, never mind surviving it when they got there. After arrival they might be clubbed to death by the natives, who Jessica and Peggy had always called Red Indians. They had learned this from the cowboy films they showed down at the 'flicks', Hale Cinema, on the corner of Willowtree Road and Ashley Road. At primary school they had frequently played games of cowboys and Indians in the playground.

The girls became aware that the immigrants were doing things like cutting down forests, destroying much-needed trees, in order to build log cabins. But there was far more to it than that; they were ruining the scenery. People don't like other people coming on to their land. They'll kill them.

Then the immigrants would begin to die in any case, of such things as malaria, typhoid and shortage of food. Catherine didn't go into all of this, just that she'd heard rumours that things were very bad. She wanted Ginger to stay in London and she wanted to go back there to make certain he did so. She was aware that other people had been trying to persuade him to go. They said that nothing was as bad as it used to be, he was only hearing about history, and that now things were a lot better organized.

"Let's go" he would say to Catherine. "We'll have a much better life there, freedom from persecution, free to be a Catholic or a Protestant."

"I'm not going."

"Well I'll go on my own."

"Please don't go!"

But indeed things were getting better. In 1620 a very different colony was established by the Puritan farmers and craftsmen. They became known as the Pilgrim Fathers, and were seeking a place where they could worship without persecution.

"You must admit that would be nice" said Ginger to Catherine.

"Oh don't go on at me!" she said, but he did, and she did too.

"Things might get better in England, there are people fighting for freedom here too."

"Not without blood."

There had been so much unrest in Oliver Cromwell's time with Puritans who seemed to think that any kind of fun, no matter how harmless, was sinful. One woman told how she actually had the soldiers inside her house, seeing if she was celebrating Christmas, telling her she shouldn't have ivy and asking her why had she got mistletoe hanging up, and had she had a man in there with her? She chased them out with a stick. That was very brave of her and she was lucky to get away with it, yet other people were getting thoroughly fed up with it, especially at Christmas time.

Things started happening. Decorations would start appearing in churches and no one would admit who had put them there. Sometimes, if they went inside people's houses to see if they were putting up such things as holly and ivy, it would be more than just one woman with a stick who would drive them back; it would be an angry crowd. Word would get around that the zealots were about.

There was also resentment about the destruction of stained glass windows in churches and statues. People wanted them back.

When the Royalists made bonfires in the street to celebrate the anniversary of the King's accession in March and got passers-by to stop to drink to his health, the Puritans couldn't stand it. There was a riot.

"Is misery their middle name?" asked Catherine. But she pointed it out that the people would eventually win out and that things would get better without emigrating. Ginger wasn't convinced and said that the passage to America was improving. He told her how the Pilgrim Fathers had left on a boat called the *Mayflower*, and they had got there all right.

"We'll go on that" he said.

"We won't! We won't go at all."

The colony flourished when the native farmers taught the settlers how to grow corn (maize), and in autumn 1621 they held their first harvest supper. They feasted on geese, turkey, duck, shellfish, watercress and wine and invited the Native Americans to the first Thanksgiving Day. Little did they know that this day would become a national holiday in the United States.

"So you see everything is lovely in America" he told her.

"No it isn't, and I don't like all this killing of animals, I won't eat them."

"Neither do I, and we will be free not to. There's lots of land to grow crops on."

He went on to say how lovely all the log cabins were, but she noticed he had said that they were of wood and that the roofs were thatched.

"People are saying that wooden houses are going to cause a fire over here, that there is going to be a big fire in London, so it'll cause them over there too."

"No there won't, they have proper chimneys made of stone or brick."

"I wouldn't be certain of that, and in any case it's all surrounded by forests, there'll be a forest fire," said Catherine.

"How old are you? You're talking like an old granny!"

"I'm not going to America."

"Life's a lot easier there."

"It's still very hard, and I'm not going."

She wouldn't give in, and neither would he.

* * * * *

Catherine could only talk about all this to the girls, as they knew where she came from. She had to be careful what she said if Grandma was in the room.

One evening they all watched television together. It was reaching the stage now where most people had a set. People were saying it was all wrong, that picture houses would soon all be closing down and that in any case it was better to go out and socialize than to stay at home and watch television. Mrs Newton remembered the first time she'd had one. She had looked out of the window and there was a young man, Mr White, walking up the path carrying it.

She had been one of the first people to have a TV. Among the others was a family who lived in Richmond Road, Bowdon, just down the road from the church school. As they had a child who attended it, Rosemary Warburton, it had attracted all the other children into the house, largely from the Vale, and they started to name the house Posh House. It was as though Rosemary had suddenly become the most popular girl in the school and her father found it very amusing, saying "Those kids need telling about going round to see someone when they want something".

One day they all went out for a game of football in the front garden. Still looking very amused, Rosemary's father looked out of the window and said, "Oh welcome to Warburton Park". These kids would sometimes go up into the loft with Rosemary. He could hear them playing above his head when he was in the room below, but it had to be stopped as he could imagine them going through the ceiling, and so could his wife Molly.

Mr Warburton later became a professor, and those kids never forgot him. He was remembered as a very nice man; that emerged when the very sad news was in the papers that he had died.

But back to Mrs Newton in 1959. She later heard there was worse to come, that televisions would all be in colour and if you had a black and white one you wouldn't be able to give it away. Next she heard that they were going to bring in remote controls. In fact that wasn't until some years later, but it was ironic that the first person she knew to have one was a woman who was notorious for being lazy.

"There won't be many people with those" she said, "it's too disgustingly lazy for anything. We can't even get up to turn over which programme we're watching. We're all going to get very fat."

One night they watched a programme about what had been done to America in the name of progress. "They can't have cut down as many trees as that" Catherine remarked, watching the screen showing countless roads with cars racing along them. The girls then realised that she had seen little more than the Devisdale, with no buildings on it whatsoever, although there was talk of it and Dunham

Wood opposite, just trees and trees. The golf course didn't come until later, and although there was the Dunham Road in between and cars racing along, there weren't many more she had seen.

Catherine was horrified by all the divorces, men and women not sticking together. It made her think she must get back to Ginger, keep an eye on him. She hoped no other girl was promising to go to America with him.

The girls both agreed with her, so the next Saturday afternoon they went to Willow Tree Cottage and climbed straight down the cellar steps as usual, to get back to 17th century London. As they went down they noticed as usual that their clothes were changing and that they were wearing again those of the period.

As they continued down, they started to feel afraid. What would they find this time? Yet when they opened the door the sun shone on them and there was the old city in front of them. Most important of all, Ginger was in front of them too. He had been walking past.

"Catherine!" he exclaimed. "Where have you been? I thought you had left me. I promise you I'll never talk about going to America again."

The pair walked off down the road side by side while Jessica and Peggy followed behind. They had a lot to talk about, but Catherine never told him she had been into the future.

Two people in the street were brawling. No one was taking any notice. Jessica and Peggy couldn't say they hadn't seen it before; they now realised it was common practice here.

They went to the baker's shop and Catherine and Ginger disappeared into the back room while Thomas Farryner, the baker, and Bessie, the servant, stayed in the shop. "Glad you've managed to get her back again" he said to Ginger.

Then he started talking about the bad old days and how he didn't want them to come back again. "What's that about?" asked Peggy, and he laughed as though he felt she already knew. She did, but he still went on to tell her more.

"You don't know how lucky you are" he said. He told her about the Puritans when he had been a young man, and how Oliver Cromwell believed everyone should live by the bible, yet it was he who interpreted what the bible said. Many inns and theatres were shut down. Women caught working on a Sunday could be put in the stocks. Even going for a walk, unless it was to church, could earn you a hefty fine. Girls had to dress in a proper manner. Make-up was banned and soldiers would roam the streets and wipe off any they found on a girl's face. Colourful dresses were banned. A Puritan lady would wear a long black dress from neck to toe, with a white apron, her hair bunched up behind a white headdress. "How absolutely awful!" said Jessica. But Cromwell hadn't stopped at that. Celebrations at Christmas were stopped and soldiers were ordered to go round the streets and take, by force if necessary, any food being cooked for the festivities.

"There was one rule for Cromwell and another for everyone else" said Bessie. "Cromwell didn't mind enjoying himself, listening to music, playing bowls and other things, and he allowed plenty of fun at his daughter's wedding."

"I bet you were glad when he went" said the girls.

"I'll say so. His son Richard had no power, so he left, and then we got Charles the Second back again. One of the first things he did was order that Cromwell's body be dug up and executed as a traitor."

Peggy and Jessica thought that was revolting and couldn't see the point of executing someone if he was already dead, but they let him go on.

"He was found guilty and his body was hanged near Hyde Park."

"I think it's horrible" said Peggy.

"No one knows what happened to his body after that. Some say it was dug up and put on a rubbish heap. His head was put on display for many years to come."

"Didn't it go off and smell?"

They were interrupted by a customer who came into the shop to buy some bread. He said that he was fed up with a man he knew who was grieving about a woman who had just died, as though there was no other woman in London. He said it was getting on his nerves. After he left Bessie remarked that one woman can't always take the place of another, and how could he be so unsympathetic? The girls remembered what their father had been like when their mother had died. However, the baker and Bessie made it clear that the customer was always right.

Then Catherine came out from the back. It was time to go. She had to go to see her mother on the other side of the city wall, so the three of them walked through the same streets.

A young girl called Elizabeth, who knew Catherine, came out of a house and invited them in. She wanted to show them a basket of puppies which had been born that day and were sitting there with their mother. One of them had already been promised to someone living down the road. They were adorable.

There was also a cat sitting very quietly on the bed next to the kitchen wall. There was a curtain hanging which sometimes went round it.

"Do you know" said Elizabeth, "The Lord Mayor is talking about getting rid of a lot of the stray dogs and cats, he thinks they will contribute to a plague."

"Well I would have thought the contrary, as they catch the rats. A lot of people say it's the rats that are causing it."

After a while they had to go, and Elizabeth joined them on their walk along the street. Music started playing. Jessica and Peggy thought it was lovely. They were told it probably meant they were getting ready for some feast for the king. Everything was so much better now, even though the people who had supported Cromwell were appalled at some of the things that had followed his death. They started saying the Stuarts were needed back again.

Elizabeth hated the city. She wanted to go back to the countryside where she had been a milkmaid. She talked of someone else who had lived there, who said he didn't like it because of the poverty and ignorance of ordinary, rural people, but he had then gone on to say that he had enjoyed the scenery and quiet life.

"The country is where I want to be" she said.

"Well you don't seem to me to be ignorant" said Peggy. and asked what she was doing there. She said she had first arrived to look after a sick relative but was now working at the hospital.

"The hospital!" They exclaimed, for they had heard such a lot about what dreadful places they were, nursing as well, and nothing to be compared with the standard of 1959. Yet it wasn't the case here, she had been somewhere run by nuns. They knew monasteries also did this sort of thing. Yet they also knew that the idea was more to keep people away from the public in order to keep them safe from catching their disease, even if it did mean they were being looked after themselves.

"I only went to get someone out" said Elizabeth. "She's not spread any disease since, in fact she's got a lot better. I think she was only put there in the first place because the relatives didn't want her any more."

She told them what she'd witnessed that day, a man having stones removed. It had been done in the home and his wife had invited Elizabeth round because she knew she assisted in this sort of thing. The poor man hadn't been allowed to get drunk first because it was an operation near the bladder. He had been tied up, and after the stone had been taken out the wound was not stitched up. It had been thought best to let it drain and heal itself. It was then washed and covered with a bandage, and this surprised Elizabeth. When she had seen it done before they kept it open at first with a small roll of soft cloth dipped in the white of an egg. In both cases the man who had the operation was fainting throughout, and then eventually he was told "All over" and Elizabeth had been waiting for them both times with a syrup drink of lemon juice and radishes.

"I heard that a much less painful way to deal with illness is to cut someone's hair off and put pigeons at their feet" said Catherine.

"And I know where you heard that" said Elizabeth. "It's how they cured the Queen when she had a fever, but it won't work for everything."

Peggy and Jessica realised that if you believe a thing then you will see it, and if a patient does get better then some people will believe such ideas really work. In fact they had met plenty of it before. They never ate meat, and anything that went wrong people would put down to this.

"Where are you living now?" asked Catherine.

"In an attic in Whitehall." They heard more music.

"I know it's good that things like this are happening since King Charles came back, but he's not a good husband at all" said Peggy. "Rumour has it that he's got a lot of other women. They should never have got rid of Charles the First. He only had one woman, his wife, and he was always a very good husband."

"That's not a good enough reason to be King of England."

They continued along the road until they came to a square where there was a market place. Girls were dancing round in a circle and holding hands. They realised that this was what the music was about, just a couple of people with musical instruments enjoying themselves.

"Let's join in" said Jessica, but Catherine said no, they should be on their way. "But I'll bring you back another time" she said.

Any joy they felt was wrecked by what came next. They were in a bear garden. The bears had had their claws and teeth removed and one was chained to a post by its neck, while dogs attacked it. Elizabeth hated it. She said a lot of people felt the same way, yet it seemed to be something they felt they had to accept, as though it was a fact of life. She said Sunday would often be a special day for it, it was like a theatre. If the poor animal died another would be brought.

As they went on their way another man who had been watching spoke to them, assuming they had all been enjoying it as he had. He told them how he had seen someone whipping a bear that was blind. It upset Jessica and Peggy, because they knew quite a bit about how some people enjoyed flogging. They had learned about it at school, and how quite a few of the Jews had died this way when Hitler had been killing them. They were shown a film about it and someone sitting at the back had let out a loud scream.

The girls moved on. They were joined by another man who had been enjoying the spectacle and talked about how he had seen a bear baited in other ways. He actually used the word 'pleasant' when describing it. He talked about how you could see the bear with its pink eyes tearing after its enemies, and how cunning and experienced the dogs were when attacking an animal so much bigger and stronger than they were. He talked about the biting and clawing, tumbling and clawing and the blood, calling it all good sport.

They all hurried on. None of them wanted to get into any sort of an argument. They came to the other side of the city wall and to the house of Catherine's mother.

"Hello, I've brought two girls with me" she said when they saw her. They were both made very welcome. Then Catherine said, "They're very shocked at the state of London".

"Oh we've had far worse than that" said her mother.

"What's that?" asked Catherine, thinking she was going to talk

39

about the rumour that there was going to be another outbreak of the plague. She had heard it so many times before. Most certainly getting out of the city was the best move for that, but it wasn't this that she was on about this time.

"Well King Charles has written to the Lord Mayor asking him to build brick houses instead of wooden ones, he fears fire damage."

"So why doesn't he do it?" asked Peggy.

A man called James came into the room. "It's not as easy as it sounds" he said.

"But we've already had some quite big fires in London and managed to get over it" said Catherine.

"Well that's all right for you, but not for everyone" said her mother. Indeed they had had fires, but none so big as some people were predicting a fire could be. Her mother went on to say that there was a lot of superstition. People had seen signs of a disaster. At Easter it had rained fish in Kent, in July egg-sized hailstones had fallen in Norfolk. The Spanish Ambassador had seen a monster with a human face, the legs of a bull, the tail of a wolf and the breast of a goat.

"They're having a dream" said Catherine.

"How can all that mean that there's going to be a fire?" hissed Jessica into Peggy's ear.

Catherine's mother went on, "It was written in a book in 1641 that a Mother Shipton, a so-called witch from York, had predicted that London will be burnt to ashes."

"Well I know religious pamphlets have been warning of a great fire, it's been going on for years" laughed Catherine.

"Oh yes" said her mother, "Ha ha indeed! Do you realise that the number 666 is the symbol of the devil and it will be 1666 next year? Do you know what these religious pamphlets say? They say God is going to send fire to London to punish Londoners for their sins, and there are plenty of them with them."

"Especially me" Catherine laughed on, but then on seeing how serious her mother was about it all she went serious herself and said, "We'll survive it".

"Not all of us."

Catherine was a governess's daughter, so she knew a bit of history. She knew, for example, that in 1649 27 barrels of gunpowder stored in a cellar had blown up, destroying 41 houses and killing 67 people. She also knew that barrels of cooking oil kept in a cellar could create a raging inferno if they caught fire, and she knew that clothes kept too close to a log or coal fire could sometimes catch light and start a blaze. A lot of people didn't like the way straw was stored in stables, and it was even sometimes laid on the floor inside the house. People were being told to use a lantern instead of a candle, especially in bed. If someone was superstitious they would wear a hare's foot around their neck as a good luck charm.

"I'm not wearing one of them" giggled Catherine.

"I will" giggled Peggy back again.

Then her mother gave her a shock. She said, "We're going to Bowdon".

"What, now?" Catherine nearly screamed. "Couldn't you have given me more notice?"

"I've not seen you for a while."

The girls settled down in the hall to toast chestnuts by the fire. Soon Catherine's mother came downstairs to say they should be getting themselves ready, but none of them needed much preparing. They were going to a place Catherine had been to many times before and anything she needed was already there.

Chapter Three

TO BOWDON BY
STAGECOACH

Jessica and Peggy thought it would be great fun to see Bowdon in 1665. Mrs Brown, Catherine's mother, didn't seem to mind them coming and they asked her if they could borrow a few things to take with them.

Shortly after, a stagecoach drew up outside the house and all five of them got in. James came too, a middle-aged man they had seen about the place.

"Poor Sally" said Catherine. Sally was one of the horses. She was getting on a bit and didn't look happy about the journey she was about to go on.

"Sally will be all right" said James. "We'll be stopping a lot to rest."

They wanted to keep the same horses and not change them on the way, as some people did. They took it all quite slowly on the road, which in places was very rocky. Jessica and Peggy had been used to smooth roads and going fast in cars.

They kept stopping for the night at inns with stables attached. How lovely it was to have a rest, and how the horses appreciated it too. It became obvious that Catherine's mother had a lot of money.

One day while jogging along, hoping to stop soon at another inn, Peggy noticed a tower in the distance. "That's Bowdon Church!" she cried out. She knew this meant that the trip would soon be over.

It wasn't long after this that they were going along a muddy track that led straight up to the church. It had big fir trees either side and they realised that they were in The Firs, then called Burying Lane, as it was the path they would take people along if they were on their way to be buried.

They were riding along full of joy when suddenly a man appeared in front of them on a horse, brandishing a gun. Then two more armed men rode from behind the firs.

"It's a robbery!" screamed Catherine, clinging to her mother.

"I'll soon sort them out" said James.

Jessica and Peggy yearned to be safe down the road at their grandmother's, but all that was 300 years into the future. One of the men got off his horse, looking extremely confident, and came towards them, pointing his gun at them. He started to open the door. Then Jessica noticed that James had also produced a gun. They screamed – there was going to be a gun fight.

They heard a sudden shot, but it did not come from James or any of the highwaymen. In fact it was one of the highwaymen who had been hit. The coach went on and more shots were fired. They noticed there was someone still among the firs pointing a gun. By now all three highwaymen were lying on the ground, dying of gunshot wounds. They assumed it was the coachman who had done it, but they were wrong.

They didn't get very far before they stopped at Church Brow, a row of small cottages at the side of Bowdon Church. Sally, the horse, couldn't take any more and the other horses were very frightened and getting restless. An old woman came out of one of the cottages and invited them in, and then a man came whistling down the road. His name was Jack; he was her son and lived there too.

They left the horses on a small patch of grass at the back of the cottages and went inside. The woman put the kettle on the fire. They realised it was Jack who had been among the firs and had fired the shots that had killed all three of the highwaymen. He told them he had seen them hanging around earlier that day and kept his eyes open, as he had guessed they were planning a robbery.

Catherine's mother gave him a sliver coin from out of her bag. Jack's mother asked him why he didn't leave it to the authorities to see to, for if they had caught them they would have erected gallows at the scene of the crime and hanged them there. Catherine and her mother knew all about that and told Jessica and Peggy about it. Shooters Hill, about eight miles out of London, was one of the most dangerous points on the Dover road; the way was steep, narrow and fringed by woods.

The girls were all told that they were to keep very quiet about it, for although the shooting had been in self-defence there could still be trouble over it. On top of this, the highwaymen might have had friends who would seek revenge.

"Well, they've left three good horses behind them" said Jack, saying he was going out to get them.

They were soon on their way again for the last part of their journey. As they jogged along Peggy and Jessica recognized a cottage and realised that they were in South Downs Road. Now it seemed an endless track, full of holes to avoid, and was so different to the way it was in the 1950s, easy to get down there on their bicycles at speed, overtaking one another with their hands behind their backs.

Finally they had arrived at their destination, a house in South Downs Road. A young woman greeted them at the door. Her name was Henrietta and she was a slight, pretty, respectable 17-year-old who had been at boarding school in Bow, a small village on the river Lea a few miles north of London. The hall was finely carpeted and it had an ornamental French clock. The kitchen was at the end of it and they noticed that there was a servant girl sitting by the fire with a baby by her side in a basket. She had her bed under the stairs and the door had to be open all the time for light.

The girls were shown their bedrooms upstairs. All three of them would share one. The beds had feather mattresses and the beds and bedsteads were obviously quite costly.

They went downstairs to dinner, finding more elaborately-carved furniture, a glass mirror and chairs cushioned with velvet. Catherine's family consisted only of Henrietta and Catherine's mother's sister Heather, whose husband was away at war. She had a twin brother, but he had recently left home and gone into lodgings.

First Sally the horse had to be seen to. She clearly knew where she was and couldn't wait to be back with her friends in the field. There was also a sheep there who had been a real old pal to her. The next day three more horses arrived, and the girls realised Jack had made some arrangement. They were the horses that had belonged to the highwaymen.

Next day they took it easy, getting up late and going for a walk around Bowdon with Henrietta. They went along a very muddy track, which was where Marlborough Road would one day be, and the boys' grammar school. The road was very wet, almost a stream, and the girls remembered how sometimes they'd heard the boys say in 1959 that a big wooden hut where they often had dances had been flooded out. As they went along they came to more streams to jump across, but at least there were springs where they could get some clean water.

They didn't go straight home but went to see friends of theirs who lived just down the road in South Downs Road; it was the house they'd been to before where there was always someone looking out of the window, and they had a daughter of 15 called Frances. They entered through a big front door and then went through the hall into the dining room, which looked into the back garden. It was a grand house with a grand hall, grand furniture and a grand staircase, yet there was nothing formal about it. Frances treated the servant girl as though she was an old pal of hers from school. They had a drop of wine, some cheese and biscuits and then went out into the back garden; it was full of bushes and trees. Jessica was pleased about that and they all ran about chasing a ball, including Emma, the servant girl, but Jessica fell over and began to giggle. She realised that the wine had gone to her head. She rolled over behind a bush, then sat upright while her head continued to spin. She knew she would soon feel better.

After a while they all went back inside the house, including Jessica, and upstairs into Frances's room. Frances started looking out of the window and Peggy asked her what she was doing, for she realised that she was the woman who was always looking out of the window.

"Oh I'm waiting for Thomas, my boyfriend, he always comes at this time" she said, and sure enough shortly after he rode up on his horse, a handsome young lad aged about 16 with a bush of blonde hair. Peggy and Jessica left, but at least they both knew who the woman was who was always looking out of the window and why she was there. She was waiting for a lover who always came.

When they arrived home they found that two old aunts had come to see them. They were talking about the good old days and about Dunham Massey and Sir George Booth.

"What a good man he was" they both agreed, and indeed he had been. He was the builder of Dunham Massey, and one of the most influential and important gentlemen in Cheshire. He was very keen on peace and quiet. He spent much of his life as a High Sheriff and Justice of the Peace, and although this gave him quite a bit of influence and power he never tried to abuse it. Nor did he try to get more power; for example, he never sought a place in the court where he would also have had more wealth.

The aunts carried on about how good he'd been to the poor. They seemed to think that quite a bit of the poverty originated from the plague in 1605 which had killed hundreds of people and had been especially bad in Chester and Stockport. But there were other ongoing problems as well that he had to see to in Bowdon and Altrincham; squabbles between tenants, drunken brawling in church, common assault and vagrants. When they got on to talking about some of the cottages that were being erected, cottages that Jessica and Peggy had seen dotted around, neither of them realised that they had to ask for special permission. "Of course they have to" laughed one of the aunts. "They can't put them there without, and even then an eye has to be kept on them, for example, there's talk of them rebuilding those cottages on Church Brow."

Sir George had also been very involved with the problems of Stockport. New taxation from King Charles I had brought about more hardship and therefore more application for relief. In 1640 it had been especially bad, and the church wardens were trying desperately hard to be fair but were very overstretched. They had 80 families on relief and had already collected £80, but when they were asked for more they had to refuse. Scroungers, and not just the needy, would ask for it. They asked Sir George for help. There was another problem; some people would harbour paupers and then use them for slave labour. It was decided to make certain they were fined.

But the worry of Stockport for Sir George didn't end there. He had received a complaint that the overseers of the poor were retaining large sums of money collected for the poor and refusing to account for it. On his authority it was decided that all village constables were to apprehend the named overseers and bring them to the next sessions to answer for their conduct.

Despite the fact that it looked very much as if there was going to be a civil war, Sir George Booth plodded on. He tried hard to reason with King Charles I, only to find him impossible. For one thing he believed in divine right and was insisting upon having a uniform Common Book of Prayer. It upset a lot of people, including William Brereton, who was a puritan, and Sir George's son in law, and it also greatly upset Sir George himself, who was a Presbyterian.

The aunts talked on, saying that even after the civil war had broken out Sir George Booth had tried not to let it affect the north, but had failed dismally, though he did manage to keep the worst of it out of Altrincham and Bowdon.

Jessica and Peggy left the room; to start off they had found it all very interesting, but now they'd had enough.

On the Sunday they went to Bowdon Church with Henrietta. How much better it was now that the Book of Common Prayer was out, or was it simply that churches vary and this was the best one Henrietta and Catherine had been to? There was nothing boring about it. The service was about forgiving other men's trespasses, showing that we should go to law and never to revenge and only repair, a good distinction.

The servant girl Mavis was full of praise, and of course it was a very good thing that the lessons all had to be in English. It was no good at all in Latin; she couldn't understand a word of it. But far more than that, she wanted to be able to read and write, and she felt as though she was getting on well with it. She had understood that all of these marks on paper stood for sounds and that you just had to put them together. It made sense; she wasn't expected to learn magic. She had mastered far more than "The cat sat on the mat". She had learned things like "I am on land" and then someone taught her the word "the", so she was able to write, "I am on the land".

She had a lot of help from one particular woman from the church who took a keen interest, and Mavis would deliberately leave pieces of paper lying about the house with little notes on them so that she could brag that she could write. But she wasn't at church that day, she had a lot to see to. Two servants had left and they hadn't got replacements yet.

After the service, Henrietta, Heather, Catherine, Jessica and Peggy went round to a friend of Heather's who'd been in church with them, only to find she only wanted them so she could talk about her troubles. She too lived in a decent-sized house with fine furniture and had servants. However, things weren't going well at all. Earlier that week she had sacked one of them, so the cook had walked out on her at a minute's notice. She got another straight away, someone who had worked in the house before, but she had forgotten or never realised that she drank, and she too left early the next morning, although she had been paid a week's wages in advance. She had left wet cloths all over the place. Then some carpenters turned up to put some new floorboards down. In all the chaos she had forgotten they were coming and wasn't prepared for it at all.

Her husband said to her, "Can't you do anything right?" and she had replied, "No, it's you who's supposed to see to these things". She hadn't been speaking to him in any case and now she was doing so even less.

After listening to her talking about it all they left and went on a walk down to Altrincham. The girls knew it would soon be time to go back to London, yet they loved this quiet place so much. At least until one night when there was a deafening racket outside. Clearly it was people who had been to some sort of a party and had too much to drink. They were merry, and singing a lot. "As long as they don't come in here" they all said.

After they had all gone past, a young woman rode by on a horse.

"She's probably had too much as well, to take a risk to be out on her own at night like that" said Heather.

Next morning they had to start thinking seriously about getting back. But there was one thing that had been troubling Jessica and Peggy, and that was the baby, Evelyn, who spent most of her time in the basket in the kitchen. She was so good and quiet and her face would light up if either of them went to pick her up or to play with her.

Henrietta told them a lot on that walk. When Jessica and Peggy had first arrived they had made the assumption that Evelyn belonged to Mavis, the servant girl, who would sit with her, only to find it was no such thing. Mavis was only 14 and had very little idea of how to look after a baby. Evelyn was in fact the illegitimate child of Heather's brother and a maid who had been in his house. It was surprising that he even admitted she was his. He didn't want the baby and had referred to her as an "ugly jade" when she'd first been born. She was now about three months old.

Peggy and Jessica were quite shocked at how few clothes the baby had on. She wore next to nothing; in fact sometimes it really would be nothing, she would just be wrapped up in a blanket. Yet she was never cold and always near the fire. They would take her sometimes into the sitting room and sit with her there in front of the fire and play. Catherine's mother made it quite clear that she couldn't take her back with her to London, and they still got shock after shock at what plans there had been for her. It seemed no one cared. She was illegitimate, a bastard, so she was despised.

Henrietta explained more as they walked on. Evelyn had been born a parish pauper in Chester, and although her father had paid a little money for her care, he didn't intend to do so for long. He had planned to give her to a beggar woman until he was warned that if she couldn't be traced he might be under suspicion for her murder. He then tried to get rid of her by giving her to a local man for £5. The man said he'd take her right out of town for him, but this only led to him going to prison for bringing a pauper child into the parish.

Peggy and Jessica were horrified. How could anyone not want the little girl? Maybe it would be different if she was a boy. Boys were treated a lot better.

"Let's see if we can get her to 1959" said Peggy. They knew there would be people in their own time who would want her.

"I'm not going all the way back on the stagecoach" said Jessica. "We can go up to the house on the Devisdale and down the steps in Willow Tree Cottage and get back that way."

"What, and then back up again and it will be Bowdon 1959? I'm not certain it will work."

Catherine said she couldn't join them as her mother would wonder where she was, so Jessica and Peggy set out on their own, carrying Evelyn in her basket. They had no trouble finding it; they knew the way from Bowdon Church and there was a muddy walk opposite, very green, which no doubt would one day be called Green Walk. As they went along they heard merry music and were thrilled to realise it was coming from the Devisdale. It made them hurry along to it.

They soon recognised Willow Tree Cottage, although it wasn't nearly so screened by trees. They were thrilled by all the merriment; there were musicians, storytellers, jugglers, minstrels, sellers of fruit and pie and acrobats. There was also a lot of dancing.

A young man stopped to talk to Peggy, introducing himself as Edward and saying he had come up from Chester, hoping to meet a girl called Emily who lived in Altrincham. He had known her for some time, although he hadn't seen her for a while. Then he began to tell her the story of his life. He had been brought up in Chester and looked after for the first few years of his life by a wet nurse. Chester was on the River Dee, a very important and prosperous port in the north west of England. His father was a wealthy merchant. They made money by selling local goods all over Europe as well as buying foreign goods to sell in England. The goods came and went in ships that sailed along the Dee.

Edward invited Peggy for some refreshments in a house in Green Walk. Peggy was fascinated by it and wondered how it had been built. He told her it had been done with wood to build the frame, and limestone for the walls. The spaces were filled with twigs and the whole of it was cemented with a mixture of powdered limestone and animal dung. It had a thatched roof. Yet it looked like a big barn to Peggy, with a ladder going up to the first floor. Did anyone live there?

Wooden shutters were used to keep out the cold as they had no glass, but she realised that this must make it very dark. He told her that sometimes they had only a fire for light. Sometimes they had candles. Edward said no one liked the thatched roof because of the danger of fire.

Peggy looked around her. Animals were everywhere. It must have been really hard work. The eggs had to be collected and the cow had to be milked. They could make cheese and butter and flour to make bread with. What they didn't need they could sell on the market. The sheep were free to graze anywhere, yet they had to keep an eye on them to make sure no one took them.

Edward didn't like the killing of animals and he had talked to Emily about it; she didn't like it either. He told Peggy she could make some lovely vegetable stews in a big iron pot that swung above the fire, and then someone would spoil it all by putting a rabbit in it.

"But don't the rabbits eat the vegetables that are growing?" said Peggy even though she didn't like it either.

"Emily says they'll find another way of dealing with that" he told her.

Any meat was collected in a pan and used to make candles with. They ate from pewter plates and drank from a cup made from the horns of a cow.

Emily, he said, had a great skill – she could spin. She could change clean wool into thread and weave it into clothes and blankets. He talked about her endlessly. "I did hope I'd meet her here" he said.

Then suddenly he saw her. He went racing out of the house on to the Devisdale calling after her, "Emily, Emily!" and she turned round to greet him. Peggy slowly went on her way, to find Jessica rushing towards her,

"Where's Evelyn?" she cried. It was a horrible moment, but one that only lasted a minute. They found that a Lady Smythe had picked her up. She adored her.

"You can have her" said Peggy.

"I will have her" said Lady Smythe. Peggy had felt that as no one else wanted her then they had the right to give her away. It reminded her rather of how people gave away cats in the 1950s.

Lady Smythe was 35 and had always wanted a child. None had been forthcoming, and then her husband was killed in the war. She was very bitter about it and lost without him. If only she could have stopped him from going. She now felt very alone in a big house in Warburton, although there were two servant girls living there as well as her. She was planning on moving to Bowdon.

"Her name's Evelyn" they told her.

"Well it's not just Evelyn now, because I'm going to call her after my mother, grandmother, and great grandmother. Her name will be Evelyn Deborah Elizabeth Margaret."

"What a mouthful to remember!"

Then the girls were startled by a voice calling "Catherine, it's time for you to go home now". It was another Catherine and another mother, but after that more mothers started arriving to take their daughters home and Peggy and Jessica realised that the party was over.

They went across to Willow Tree Cottage and realised it was occupied, so they knocked on the door. A middle-aged woman came to the door.

"We want to go to London. Can we take a short cut through your cellar?"

"You've had too much to drink, go home."

"We haven't and we know we can get to London very quickly that way."

"What cellar?"

A man came to join her, and Peggy told him, "There is a cupboard in your house and some stone steps leading down from it."

"I know that. but they don't lead to London" laughed the woman.

"They do!"

"Now buzz off!" said the man and closed the door on them. They wandered slowly back to the house on South Downs Road. Now they knew there was only one way back, and that was a long one, in the stagecoach.

They were surprised when they got there that everyone was horrified to learn Evelyn had gone.

"She's gone to Lady Smythe's in Warburton" Jessica told them. "She'll soon be moving to Bowdon."

They went straight back to see the baby, but not to get her back. Lady Smythe said that she would pay someone to come and look after her and so they left it at that. It seemed that she had found a good home.

Now it was time to go back to London. They left Sally in the field to retire and took another horse instead. Just as they were going a young, fair-haired lad went inside the house.

"His mother won't be very pleased to see him" said Mrs Brown. The girls didn't know who he was. She told them he was Henrietta's twin brother, Heather's son. She had turned him out, as he had revolted. He had stayed out late, become too friendly with the maid, corrupting her, according to his mother, and getting drunk. He had refused to go to church. He wore his hat in the house and flung his coat dramatically over his shoulder in the street like a ruffian.

There was a coach service that went regularly to London from Manchester but no one wanted to take it, they wanted to be able to take their own time and somehow if they could do that it didn't seem so long. Their journey was a quiet one and they were glad to be back home again.

Catherine's mother got her to talk on her own about baby Evelyn.

"Catherine, I know I should have done more about that child, but to be truthful I didn't even know about it until I went up there this last time" she said. "I was quite afraid. I had such a time when you were born, even though you had a good father."

"But would you have allowed her to go to a beggar woman? She just wanted her so that she could get more money begging with a child."

"I wouldn't have done, yet I don't know what I would have done, men can vary so much and my brother is nothing like your father. I was just so relieved when I found out how dedicated Lady Smythe was."

"But you have money. You could have hired someone, as Lady Smythe did."

"I couldn't. I haven't got much control over the money I have. It's a great shame that your father died. It seems all the good people die young."

Catherine then went out to look for Ginger, but she couldn't find him anywhere. Perhaps he'd left her. She couldn't believe he'd do that, but she couldn't wait any longer, as Jessica and Peggy were talking about going back to Bowdon and she wanted to go with them.

Just as they were going, her mother said to her, "There are other things I want to speak to you about."

"Sorry, I'm off!" said Catherine.

They left. Catherine said, "You know my mother will go on at me like this. She wants me to get out of the city because she's so certain that the plague is on the way, yet when an old friend of hers came up to see her, they played cards with the servants, went out shopping with her, went on the river together and visited old haunts. She likes London herself."

"It's in the house where you once lived isn't it?"

"Yes, but she doesn't want me back, she's too afraid of the plague. In the last few decades there have been some outbreaks and they're always in the city."

They walked towards the door, keen to get back to 1959 on the Devisdale, but as they went through it Ginger arrived. She was so pleased to see him, yet she had to go.

"I can't stay just now either" he called back to her. "We're like passing ships."

"We won't always be" she said, and they threw each other kisses. Catherine walked through the door with the girls and up the cellar steps.

Before going home they went to see a friend in Bow Green Road and took a short cut down an alleyway by Bowdon Church. Jessica let out a shriek.

"Look at that tombstone!" she said. It's Evelyn's."

It was indeed. The inscription stated that the grave was of Evelyn Deborah Elizabeth Margaret, an old woman who had died in 1740 and been buried with Lady Smythe and a servant girl, presumably the one hired to look after her. "I think we can now say that Evelyn had a good life" said Peggy, and they all agreed.

Mrs Newton was pleased to see them. She told them about a Harry she knew and had been talking to that day.

"He says it's getting on his nerves that a friend of his is grieving for a woman who has died and says it's as though there's not another woman in Bowdon" he said.

"Another woman won't take her place" said Jessica. Mrs Newton agreed, and said he was very hard. The girls kept looking at one another as they remembered the same conversation taking place in the baker's. "It's no better these days" they thought.

Chapter Four

LIFE WITH MRS NEWTON

When Christmas came, Jessica and Peggy went away with their grandmother to a house where they were all vegetarians and called themselves a vegetarian community. The trouble they found was that vegetarians or vegans were a wide cross-section of people, and if you meet a lot of them then some will be most unpleasant characters. They certainly found this here.

Another problem was that Mrs Newton wasn't keen on men, as some of them had a problem with fearing or hating women. She knew that some people believed that you should only use the word fear, it wasn't hate, but she could not always accept that, if they were aggressive and devious.

She certainly found this with one of the men there. This man was evil. She had met a lot of nice Polish men, but this one was an exception. He was nicknamed Jolly and his wife, also Polish, was nicknamed Dolly. She was a very good-looking woman who could speak hardly any English. She was also extremely nervous and spent nearly all her time upstairs in her room. When she was downstairs she had a silly sort of giggle about her and would be like a doll in a glass box on the fairground. Mrs Newton, who had some experience in teaching foreigners to speak English, was very happy to help her with this, but she had to stop because Jolly clearly didn't like it. She wondered if he was being nasty when he said, "You're like a schoolteacher". She wondered why he didn't teach her himself, as he taught English in a school in Poland. However, her lack of English did mean he had extra control over his wife. Keeping people ignorant in order to exert control is far from unheard of. In South Africa they used to flog anyone who tried to teach a black man to read and write.

When the couple were talking in Polish together Mrs Newton could hear her name mentioned, accompanied by this girl's silly giggle. She didn't like it much, although she certainly didn't intend to complain about it. She did once say "What's the joke?" He told her, and they were indeed sneering at her. Maybe he enjoyed letting her know that. If he was trying to get a row going between two women, that would be a symptom of misogyny, men who hate women.

That evening she was in the kitchen making herself a cup of tea when the giggling was going on, but she decided to ignore it. She would have her cup of tea in the next room and it didn't trouble her all that much. However, Jolly wasn't going to let her do that, and as she was leaving the room with the cup of tea he insisted on knowing what she was looking so serious about. She didn't think she did look particularly serious, but she did say that she didn't know what the joke was. He caused no end of trouble and went upstairs to the manager to complain. The manager backed him to the hilt and came downstairs especially to tell her that she shouldn't be so sensitive.

She was shocked that Jolly had said he was amazed that she should think the jokes were about her, because not only could she hear her name being used, he had admitted to it. However, it is typical of a misogynist to say he's amazed that someone should think he's done such a thing when he has. He was implying that she was just a silly bitch. She also felt certain that if she had refused to tell him what she looked serious about, he would have caused trouble about that.

The manager told her he had two men to support him, so it was four men in all against one woman, and it is typical of a misogynist to get several men to agree with you against one woman. But the two other men who agreed with the manager and Jolly turned out to be of such bad character that she later thought they didn't count. She left next day crying and they were very happy to see her go. There was no thanks to her for stopping a big row breaking out by doing this, and it was a lot of trouble she went to.

When she got back home she found everyone strongly supported her, although none of them knew much about misogyny in those days. One Polish woman apologized to her about it and two others told her that as Jolly had been in the country some time, he would have known that the English frequently don't like them speaking a foreign language and so he would have known he might well be causing a lot of trouble.

How could Mrs Newton be so certain that he was doing it? She got it tape recorded and the two Poles translated it for her. She was very lucky that there was a tape recorder in the house as they were rare in those days and that Jessica knew how to work it, but it was so. It's not against the law to do this – it's what you do with it afterwards, and they were all taking care of this. They felt that Mrs Newton had the right to know what was being said about her.

Why was he doing all this? Had he found Mrs Newton a threat

because she was so willing to help his wife to understand the language? The two Poles wrote a letter between them to the girl in Polish, saying that although she had the support of four men everyone else supported Mrs Newton. They were both very educated people who would know how to write a gentle and tactful letter, and were well aware that her giggling would only be because she was so nervous.

However, maybe they should have known that the girl wouldn't be allowed to see it. Jolly thought he owned her in the same way you own a car, a symptom of misogyny. No doubt it was in the name of caring that he didn't let her see the letter. He said it was an attacking one, which it was not. In fact it couldn't have been less so. We cannot know if the girl was being awkward or not because she could not speak English. Everything had to be channelled through him, and although there was a bad report on her later about something else it all originated from Jolly, who had started up the most dreadful rumours about her, and she was not in a position to defend herself.

* * * * *

"Will you girls stop talking about boys!" Mrs Newton said as they all settled down in front of the television to watch a programme about the war. It showed the Blitz and London on fire. How well Mrs Newton remembered it, and oh how she wanted to talk about it, but the girls had heard so much of it already from their other grandmother, who had died when they were ten. First you would hear the sirens going, so you would know the Germans were coming, and you would rush to the air raid shelter. Then you would hear their planes arriving. That would be followed by the sounds of guns going off, which would be the British shooting them down. It was terrifying.

"Grandma wasn't afraid" said Jessica. "She was shooting them down."

"Oh, don't exaggerate" said Mrs Newton.

"Well, you were floodlighting the skies so that the people who were shooting at them could see them."

"Not me, it was the young girls doing that, girls who should have been out rocking and rolling with some of those young pilots. They shouldn't have been shooting and killing one another."

She said that their father, along with the rest of the men who were shooting the planes down, had had a magnifying glass at the side of his gun, so after the sky had been lit up as bright as daylight they could also see them as big as big could be. They then started flying dangerously low, and the British would be flying just as low over Germany when they were bombing the enemy. It made it a lot more difficult to shoot them down and it also meant they wouldn't hear the sirens going off, as they would miss the radar. The Germans were also making the most dreadful screeching noise, in order to frighten everyone and sap their spirit, and probably the British were doing the same back to them. It wasn't unusual, especially in Kent, for a German pilot to land.

"I wish some of those pilots would start parachuting down on Bowdon now" said Peggy.

"Would be nice" Catherine remarked, wishing Ginger would suddenly drop down from out of the sky.

"Well, there was a prisoner of war camp in Dunham Wood" their grandmother told them.

"So it was nice" said Catherine. She then started talking about the wars England kept having with Holland during the 17th century.

"The Dutch were coming up the River Thames" said Jessica, who had gone to look it up.

"I never said that!" said Catherine.

"They attacked Medway Harbour."

"When?"

"1667."

"Well, that was after the plague." Meaning of course that she was dead by then, so she wouldn't know about it.

Mrs Newton joined in. "We've always been having wars with Spain, Holland or Germany. We've had three wars with Germany in the last hundred years. Who will it be next?"

"Russia."

Then Mrs Newton went back to talking about when the prisoner of war camp had been in Dunham Wood and how the prisoners would go to the public house in Bowdon, the Stamford Arms. She went on to explain how girls who went with the enemy were considered absolute sluts and how after Germany was defeated in France, they shaved all their hair off and paraded them through the streets on open lorries.

"But that was different. Wasn't it because the Germans were occupying it, they weren't their prisoners?"

"What were you doing out in the Blitz in any case?" asked Catherine. Mrs Newton had been in the Red Cross and had come out sometimes when she was not supposed to. She talked about the Home Guard, how everyone was afraid of them and if you showed a light you could get into trouble. The Germans must not be allowed to know where the cities were. Yet at times they had come to get her if someone was injured.

After a raid, Queen Elizabeth, later to become the Queen Mother, would come out to talk to the people and keep their spirits up. Catherine was pleased that there was still a Royal Family. She had some sort of a feeling that they were divine and that it would be punishable by God to get rid of them. She remembered how she had heard her mother talking about how glad they were when King

Charles was restored to the throne and that they hoped this meant
God would forgive some of them, for his father, Charles the First, had
had his head cut off. She could remember quite clearly people talking
about the Civil War in the same way Jessica and Peggy had heard
everybody talking about the war with Germany, for they had been
born in it, evacuated to Wales, and were only two when it finished.

"I would love to see London now" said Catherine.

"Oh, it's nearly all built up since the fire."

"What fire?"

"The fire, London was on fire during the Blitz in 1940" said Mrs
Newton. Yet it wasn't the same as the Fire of London in 1666. True,
it was the same noise and falling buildings, but fewer than ten people
died and it only lasted a few days. It did leave people suffering though,
booksellers especially. Some books were put into churches for safety,
only to find the church burned down. It took a long time to build up
again.

Jessica and Peggy knew that neither London nor Altrincham had
been completely built back up after the Blitz. They remembered being
very young and going to Stamford Park with their mother and being
told they were not allowed to pick the flowers, nor were they allowed
to pick them out of people's gardens. Yet there was one park they were
allowed to go into and pick as many flowers as they liked. A few years
later one of them questioned her mother about this. It seemed strange
that she had allowed her to do it. It turned out that it wasn't a park
but a bomb site. A house in Byrom Street was bombed when the
Germans were aiming for the railway lines, and there was another
place in Altrincham which was bombed, on the corner of Moss Lane
and Oakfield Road. There was a memorial there in memory of 14
people who were killed there.

Catherine got back on to the subject of the civil war during the
17th century. She could only go by what she'd heard people say, but

they said plenty. There hadn't been much fighting on the streets of London. There had been plenty going on around the Houses of Parliament and the River Thames, which wasn't far from where she'd been born. There had been scuffles all right – maybe that was an understatement, Members of Parliament had been forcibly thrown out. In 1642 Charles the First had pursued five MPs who he was trying to arrest, but he was mobbed by tradesmen, apprentices and seamen, all shouting "Privilege of parliament, privilege of parliament!" It was a mouthful for them, but they made it sound threatening.

Catherine's mother had been present, and she felt afraid. Which side should she take? Would she be expected to take either? She ran inside. Meanwhile the king knew he had lost control and left London the next week. The day after he'd gone the MPs he'd threatened made a triumphal journey on the Thames from the City of Westminster, escorted by boats carrying waving and cheering Londoners. Catherine's mother was no longer afraid to come out. She joined them as she walked along the side of the river, feeling safe in a crowd. Soldiers marched along the strand with drums and flags to greet the MPs when they came ashore.

The next big street show was the execution of two Catholic priests in front of an approving crowd. Catherine's mother was glad she didn't see that. In March Parliament began to raise its own army. It ordered the digging of trenches and forts to close down all main roads to London. A huge workforce was needed for this, and it included women and children. Catherine's mother joined in. When announcements were made in the churches, people turned up with baskets and spades and suchlike, thousands of them. They were directed by sailors and officers of a trained band. It kept the royals out, yet there were still fears that Prince Rupert might come.

If Mrs Newton was in the room, Catherine took care to make it sound as though it was all very much history to her; something she'd read in a book and not something that happened in her childhood. Their grandmother told her how Prince Rupert had stopped on the Downs with his army of men, on his way to win Chester back again for the Royalist, but he soon marched on to Cheadle and the enemy immediately retreated. Four years later a meeting of Lieutenancy was held in Bowdon and plans were made to recruit more men, but without success. The locals didn't want to enrol under the banner of the King. It is recorded in Didsbury Library that he was there.

Mrs Newton went into the kitchen to do the washing up while the three girls got on with their chatter. They were telling Catherine how they would teach her to ride a bicycle, and she definitely wanted to as she got more used to the traffic. She was beginning to think of it as something exciting, riding something herself.

The telephone rang, but none of them noticed until their grandmother came rushing into the room. "Your father's in prison, your father's in prison!" she cried. She had planned on quietly explaining it all to them should this happen, but when it did she found she just couldn't manage it.

The girls looked horrified, most of all Catherine. She said, "What, has the bell told you that?" for although she had heard them talking on the phone before and knew that such a thing was possible, she was finding it a lot to swallow. And then, almost crying, she talked as though prisons were as bad as those in the 17th century and even brought up the subject of the Tower of London. The grandmother was touched that someone who didn't know her very well could show such concern, as it showed how grateful she was, or at least it had made her feel some warmth towards her.

The girls started saying, "Where has he been all this time?" but Mrs Newton didn't answer. No one was certain when exactly they had last seen him.

Catherine started getting upset. "Oh stop all this!" she said.

"When did you last see your father?" She felt that there was something sinister about it, as though it reminded her of something, but she didn't know what. Mrs Newton clearly thought so too. "I didn't mean it to sound like that" she said.

"When did you last see your father?"

Catherine felt she had to go. No one tried to stop her. She strolled sadly across the Devisdale that evening back to Willow Tree Cottage, and knew it might be difficult to go back to that house again. In a crisis like this a family like to be on their own.

When she got in she lay on top of the camp bed. She could hear the birds singing and there was a fox just outside; if only life could always be as peaceful as this. She began to doze off. She began to dream, about the Civil War; she was in a house with some Royalists. Some soldiers had been and spoken to the little boy, but his mother had spoken to him first. She had got him on his own and told him, "Don't you tell them your father was here the other night." He said he wouldn't. She went into it with him, how they would tell him that if he should tell a lie he would be punished by God, but this wasn't true at all. He vowed he wouldn't tell them a thing, and nor did he. The Royalist family were captured by Parliamentarians and the child was cross-examined by them in front of a panel, but he stuck to his story, he had not seen his father. He later justified it, but only when it was very safe to do so, by saying he really hadn't, it had been so dark that all he had seen was some kind of a shadow.

She was woken from this dream by the noise of some children playing; a mother was calling across to them, "Have you seen your father?" She got up from the bed and lit the oil stove camp fire, just one ring. The girls had given it her. She made herself a hot drink. She needed time to think.

Jessica and Peggy did come to see her a few days later. They were horrified by what they found. Louts were throwing stones at the cottage. They wondered how they knew it was there, when so many people denied it existed. A bottle narrowly missed Peggy's head as she rushed past them all and into the tree, Jessica following.

They found Catherine hiding against the wall in case they started to invade the place. When she saw them she started to cry out to them, "Oh they've been shouting, "Witch, witch, come out of there you horrible old witch!"

The three of them ran down the cellar steps to get to London, but when they opened the door they found it was even worse down there. Whatever was going on? It seemed they were taking someone through the streets to be executed. The crowds were fighting, some saying it was wrong and others saying it should go ahead.

"I can't stay here!" Catherine cried out, and the three of them raced up the stairs and found themselves back in the cottage. They sat down on the floor leaning up against the wall. At least the mob from outside had gone. Then they started on their way back to Mrs Newton's, but Catherine felt she couldn't stay there long.

It was Peggy who was most traumatized. "Oh it's horrible, horrible!" she cried out. She seemed to know what it was, but then she had strange powers.

"What was it?" asked Jessica

"They were taking a woman through the streets to be burnt as a witch."

"They weren't!" said Catherine. They went straight upstairs and into the bedroom. Catherine asked Peggy why she was so very afraid.

"I've got strange powers. I'm the sort of person that would be burnt as a witch."

"You may have strange powers but you have guessed this wrong, the days are going fast when they do that, it's fading into history for me, and it was in my mother's time."

They got out a book to look it up. Although they did find that burning women as witches was fast going out in the 1660s, it nevertheless upset Peggy very much that she'd been in a place where it had happened so recently. She wondered how they could be so unfair as she read on, but she had learned at school how even these days, in some countries, they still have kangaroo courts.

They talked more about what had happened in old England, for Catherine's mother had worked for someone called William who had had some influence in getting the poor suspect released. He couldn't stand it. They had such strange ideas on what "evidence" they needed to "prove" that a woman was a witch. A "familiar" could be any kind of an animal, although the first one which came to mind was a black cat. If a mouse, fly or spider crawled into the cell where the suspect was being held, then it could be claimed it was her familiar. It was believed to be created by the devil, to help the witch carry out her evil work. It was also believed that a witch's familiar would feed off her blood, and this would cause marks on her skin which were called devil's marks. Any scar or boil or spot might be pounced on and called a devil's mark. They weren't difficult to find. A lifetime of hardship, a poor diet and bad teeth could so easily cause scars, boils and mouth ulcers. Yet all the time while they were reading it, Catherine kept saying, "Those days are going."

"I wonder if they were taking someone to be hanged, drawn and quartered" said Peggy.

"No" said Catherine, "I'm sure it was no more than a lot of brawling, it was nothing unusual."

But they did go back to the subject of women being accused of being witches, and again it reminded Peggy and Jessica about some of the things they'd read in the newspapers in some faraway countries and their mad, mad trials. It also said that some of the women confessed to it.

"Why on earth would they do that?" said Peggy.

69

"They may have been up to something even if they weren't witches" said Jessica.

"No they hadn't" said Catherine, "they were tortured. They would keep the suspect standing up, and walk them up and down until their feet blistered. They would never get any sleep, and they would humiliate them by forcing them to stand naked while they were being questioned. It would get so that they would agree to anything."

Mrs Newton knocked on the door, aware that something stressful was going on. "Can I come in?" she said.

"Of course you can."

"Are you coming down to tea now?"

They changed the subject over tea, and when they'd finished Catherine said she had to go. She could see that they wanted to be on their own as there was a lot going on as regards their father. She was right about that, yet Jessica and Peggy told her before she went that they would find some solution to everything.

When it became dark she walked into Altrincham, and she didn't go back. She spent quite a few nights sleeping rough, and would sometimes think of even moving on from Altrincham. The grass would be greener on the other side, but when it came to it she'd soon forget it. It would mean leaving a place she knew and going into the unknown with nothing to protect her. Not likely. At least in Altrincham some people were pleasant. She didn't want to be near to people who could be so hard or even violent, which was what she had heard about some places, especially London. Homeless people could be attacked in their sleep or even knifed, just for a few coppers or their sleeping bag. You were just another dosser and already, where she was, she had been verbally attacked quite badly more than once. One man had said to her, "You're standing in the right place" meaning she was by the rubbish bin, and yet that was where she was going to stay. She found it unbelievable what people threw away; she could soon go through the bins and get out some food.

At times it stopped her having to beg. People would come up to her and say, "Go and buy yourself something nice" and push a coin into her hand. In fact she found she had no need to beg at all.

Sleeping rough made her even scruffier, even though she had been given more clothes, for she was now sleeping in them. She began to think about London again, as she was finding Altrincham could be tough. She would frequently hear people say "Put her in the army." They assumed she was drinking, or never did any work. Didn't they realise the army wouldn't want her if she was like that? She didn't know if the army would want her in any case. She hated it that she was considered such trash.

Yet at the same time, some people were sympathetic. People were telling her she might find it better in London, as there were more facilities for the homeless. She couldn't imagine how it could be as she had only seen it in the 17th century. She could only think about the plague and yet they'd go on telling her it was the place where it all happened, a place full of opportunities and somewhere you could be anonymous, no one asked you where you came from, and even if they did you could move on or invent your own past.

But she remained in Altrincham. She loved to hang around the big clock just outside the station. It was a meeting place for young lovers, and she would see them there night after night. She would get so close sometimes she could hear proposals of marriages, and she dreamt about Ginger coming and joining her there. It seemed to be that it didn't matter if you went to meet someone who didn't turn up, because there was bound to be someone else who had been stood up. But she only wanted Ginger.

As night fell she would go on looking for a doorway. She found a good deep one in Regent Road. It was so deep that the light from the street lamps and shop front didn't reach the door itself and she could sit with her back against it and not be seen by a passer-by. It was ten at night and she was eating a bread roll watching various people going by, but no one looked her way. She began to think about rolling up in her sleeping bag, for she knew she had to be up early and away before the shop opened. She was finding she could do this every night, until she got there once and found someone else there. "Here, I was here first" she said.

"Tough, you're not here now" came a man's voice, very rough, hidden deep inside a sleeping bag. She knew she didn't stand a chance. She walked away with a lump in her throat. How long would this go on? Was she going to spend the rest of her life being pushed about? How long was she going to live for? Perhaps she'd live for ever.

The next night she went to the same spot, but he was there again. This time he was just sitting on the step for everyone to see. He had taken her place from her. As she strolled off she heard a scream and turned round. He had grabbed someone's wrist and was saying "Nice little watch" to them.

She ran away, shouting, "That man there is robbing someone!" People started running towards him, but she ran away. What would he do to her if he found out it was she who had raised the alarm?

She didn't go to that shop doorway again. She soon found another one in George Street which was just as deep; she clung to her sleeping bag and hoped this wasn't someone else's bedroom. Yet she was so tired she just got her head straight down. She was woken up by someone pushing her out, and panicked. Perhaps it was that man again, or perhaps it was another big man. Perhaps it was someone who fancied her, how horrible!

In fact it was a young girl. She tried to push her away, saying "I was here first". The girl didn't argue, but she didn't go either. Catherine gave her another push, to find that she was lying on a soft mattress. She pushed her right off it and settled on it herself. The girl was very drunk and soon began to snore. She slept on the stone floor.

Very early the next morning they were both woken up by someone very kind, who gave them a full picnic basket. The two of them sat up straight to eat it. Having nothing to eat makes you quarrelsome; having something to eat soothes everything.

Another night she heard footsteps, not too heavy, yet she found them formidable. She trembled. Was it the big man come to take her place? She prayed they would go straight past, but they didn't. A torch shone in her face. She tried to hide; she wanted to run. She realised that whoever it was, they could see her but she couldn't see them. She got closer and closer to the door, still only sitting up in the forlorn hope that someone would come to it from the inside and open it so that she could escape.

Then a woman's voice, soft and gentle, told her, "It's all right, this is the police". Catherine wondered what she called 'all right'. Would she be taken down to the police station? Would they put her into a police cell? Would they ask her who she was? How could she tell them she was someone from the 17th century who had climbed out of a mirror? But the policewoman merely added, "You will have to be away from here before the shop opens" and walked on.

The next night, same place, someone else came to join her, a man. "Don't worry, I just want to roll this joint" he said. She didn't realise it, but a big drug problem was beginning all over the world.

"Been on it long?" she asked him.

"Seven months."

She realised he was in a much bigger mess than she was.

"I can tell where you come from" she said, meaning that his accent was a London one.

"And I shan't be going back there."

"Don't you recommend me to go?"

"No." He rolled his joint and went.

The next time she was woken up by someone, it was a man nudging her and saying, "Come on love". She looked up and he stood back. It was a police officer. He moved her on.

She managed to get something to eat straight away. A woman called Veronica had seen it all from a late-night coffee house and took her inside to buy her a meal. Catherine found out that there were some kind people around as well as bad.

"Take care when talking about where you can go" Veronica warned her. "Don't give them the chance to say you deliberately made yourself homeless, they have no obligation to find you anywhere to live if they can say that." She also went on to say that they sometimes say kids trick people into giving them money when they have a home, and then go back to it with some cash they've begged for, which they spend on cigarettes and alcohol.

"But I don't beg. I've never asked anyone to find me a home and I don't smoke nor drink" said Catherine.

She went to another doorway that night on Kingsway, hoping that the same police officer wouldn't come along. A cold wind was blowing up, and it went right through her. She decided to walk about instead. She felt a lot warmer, as she'd had plenty to eat. The daylight started coming in and people started passing on their way to work.

A tramp was walking ahead of her, asking everyone he passed, "Have you got any change?" She began to study people's response. Some would stare straight ahead as though they hadn't heard. One man said "Can't go out anywhere without being asked for money". Another said "What change, I'll soon change you." But mostly they would just look angry.

She wondered if she should go back to the garage at Mrs Newton's. Couldn't any solution be found? Anything was better than this, as long as it wasn't London.

She decided to give it a try at Frances's in South Downs Road; maybe she could find somewhere comfortable there. She wandered up the path and sure enough, Frances was standing at the window looking out.

"Frances, can I come inside and have somewhere comfortable to lie down?" she called up to her. She heard her answer, her voice so soft and gentle. "I can't, Mrs Lomax here is already very frightened of me, I try to stop her seeing me."

"But Frances, can't you explain it all to her?"

"She'd never understand" she said, and at that moment Mrs Lomax came to the door looking the same as before, scruffy and wearing an overall and more as though she was a worker there than the owner of the house. She had her sleeves rolled up.

"What do you want?" she demanded.

"I'm talking to Frances, she means no harm," Catherine muttered nervously.

"Well if you mean no harm either just shift, will you, and there's no one called Frances round about here or anyone else, I live on my own."

Catherine ran for it, but as she did so, although she couldn't see anything, she could hear the noise of a horse trotting; maybe it was Thomas coming to see Frances. She was waving to someone out of the window.

She felt quite nervous as she walked up Stamford Road. No one saw her go into the garage. When she got there she found the same camp bed and blankets waiting. She lay down and slept for hours. She was woken up by the girls, who were very pleased indeed to see her. She was very hungry, so they all went inside for a big fry-up. As regards the father, they had been told that they would just have to wait until he'd done his time and then think about what to do next.

They still wanted to visit him in prison and to write to him regularly. Meanwhile he wanted them to plod on as usual as far as possible, and this they did, but there was another scare; there was an outbreak of polio and people in Altrincham were getting it. There were warnings about it everywhere, about how it spread, especially in cinemas. They had been waiting for a film to come to Hale, but their father forbade them to see it. They didn't dare go; someone might see them there and it would get back to him.

Then a little later after all the scare, they heard some good news. Johnny Ray, their pop idol, was coming to Belle Vue in Manchester. Mrs Newton said she'd take them to see him and the three of them went together. There had been trouble at such places, girls dancing in the aisle, swinging their full skirts about, showing plenty of lacy petticoats, some leg and maybe even suspenders, so now they were making certain everyone sat quietly in their seats. Even when the girls went with Mrs Newton to the toilet they were questioned by the usherette as to where they were going. But all wasn't quiet as Johnny Ray crooned away one love song after another; in fact he was nicknamed "Cry Ray" because his songs were so much about women deserting him. Girls just screamed away, but not Peggy or Jessica. They just sat next to Grandma, quietly enjoying it all. Two girls who sat behind them cried through it all. At one point he was leaning over the stage having a necking session with a girl on the front row.

A few weeks after that he was arrested for being a homosexual. It was illegal in those days. It wasn't that either of the girls were put off by it, they just lost interest. All hope is gone if a man is homosexual, although it may have been a blessing in disguise to him. They were told he retired shortly after this and had a quiet life doing nothing but playing the piano in a night club.

"Oh that's what he calls a quiet life!" said Mrs Newton. "Well I wouldn't like to have what he calls a noisy life then."

The girls were quite shocked at what she seemed to know about;

it was as though she'd once been in a club like that herself. She talked about people having to be thrown out of some of these places and the police having to be called. She even seemed to imagine that he himself might have to join in some of the struggles.

"The pianist won't be expected to!" exclaimed the girls.

"Won't be expected to, no, but sometimes they can't help it if muscle power is needed and bar staff are being overpowered, you can even get customers having to join in."

They then heard how in show business it was common knowledge that Ray was a homosexual and none of them could imagine how it hadn't got out sooner. The word "gay" hadn't come in yet; it still merely meant very happy. As it was illegal they had to keep it to themselves. "Gay" was their secret language.

Then they went to see a girl they had been at primary school with, Helen, who lived in Stockport. They went to the market just by St. Mary's church to get some records, which were going very cheap. Gramophones really fascinated Catherine; she'd spend some time winding them up in order to hear more music. She found it unbelievable that such a thing could work, that music had been played so far away and so long ago and yet you still could hear it.

While she was standing at the stall Peggy's head started to spin and she realised she was fainting. She clung onto a table cloth in order to try to make herself steady but this only made things worse, and as she went down on to the ground she took all of the crockery with her, which landed on the ground with a huge crash.

When she opened her eyes again she found that that the whole of the market place had changed and it was now half way up a hill. Although she realised it must have been there before, it hadn't been so obvious with all the buildings around it; now there were hardly any. She was in the country.

She looked up and saw a big house called "Staircase House". It looked daunting. She looked down and saw a straggling hilly town divided by fields and gardens. She felt completely lost. Then a voice called from behind her "What are you doing here?"

She turned round and saw coming out of the big house a middle-aged woman in very fine clothes dating from around the 16th century. Peggy felt afraid, but the lady gently said to her "Come inside, you haven't got the plague".

When Peggy looked down she noticed that although shabbily dressed, she too was in clothes dating back to the 16th century.

The house became more daunting as she entered it. She was in a grand passageway and although it was not a big one, there was a fine staircase in front of her. The lady who took her in was called Mrs Shawcross and this wasn't her only home, the Shawcrosses had another mansion in Derbyshire. Peggy was led into another room and noticed from the window some fine pasture land that went down to the river. There were animals grazing on it, was called Shawcross's Fold and it belonged to the family.

"How bad is the plague?" Peggy asked her.

"Oh, thirty or forty people have it. I can't see it getting any worse in Stockport, they say it only spreads in places where it's crowded."

"What year is it now?"

"1605."

"So the great plague of London hasn't happened yet?"

Mrs Shawcross laughed and said, "I can't tell the future! Don't worry, no one is going to send you away."

She imagined Peggy was getting it mixed up with The Black Death in 1347 which swept through everywhere, including Altrincham and Stockport. Indeed it was after this that peasants realised that their labour could be quite valuable, so they travelled about. Landowners would pay them good wages, but the ruling classes started passing laws that said they had to be sent back to their parish of birth or be beaten and put in the stocks as vagabonds. So much depended on luck and whether or not the crops were plentiful or failing. Yet for some time there had been some kind people around. Annuities were left by wealthy men, for example, Edmund Shaa, whose will was dated 1488, left money to start up a free grammar school in Stockport, and appealed for help for the poor people in the town. Still there was always the problem of scroungers abusing it. The first poor law had only just been passed, in 1601, but Mrs Shawcross's only interest was in Peggy, for she was a very kind person.

Peggy went downstairs into a basement. Now she could see the cattle and dogs she had heard. They were in the back part of the stable and seemed to treat it as though it was their home.

"I love animals" she said.

"In that case you must stay and look after them" said Mrs Shawcross, and a straw mattress was brought down with some woollen blankets and put on the stone floor for her. Peggy sat on it. It seemed comfortable enough. She was used to the country, to things like camping, sleeping in barns and being among the animals, yet she hoped she wouldn't be there for long, for she knew that soon she would be yearning to go back to the life of Bowdon in 1959.

As the days went by, other things happened to make her very unhappy. She was living in this basement on a stone floor with stone walls, which were very good for preserving the food in the next room, for example the fruit, but it was very uncomfortable for her. She didn't like it either that the animals had to be slaughtered before the winter set in. They said it was because it was difficult to preserve so much of the meat for so long, and she wondered why they ate it at all. Why couldn't they just live off the land? Especially as people who didn't eat meat were so much healthier. Yet she said nothing, hoping they weren't noticing that she never ate any herself. She knew she was in the hands of some very kind people.

She helped out in the next room, where she had to rub salt into the flesh of dead animals. It disgusted her. "Won't all this salt spoil the taste of meat?" She asked a young lad who worked with her. He told her they would be adding various herbs to it and in any case the cook could always put it into a stew with a lot of other spices. When she asked him why they couldn't have just a stew of spices and herbs he laughed. He said that of course you had to eat meat. She thought again about their health. All this salt wouldn't be doing it any good.

Then shortly after, Robert Aulton, the respected butler, walked in wearing a very smart suit which had been left him in a will. He had already noticed that Peggy wasn't very happy, so he told her she could go upstairs and work in the kitchen. When she got there she found it no better, as she had to deal with dead birds.

"Oh, leave them alone to fly free!" she would think. She wondered again why they didn't just live off the land and have a plant-based diet instead of eating flesh, more so when she heard them complain about the transport being bad and how they depended upon it for meat. She had seen the horses and wagons arriving in the courtyard when she had worked in the basement below. It seemed that if something was difficult to get or if it was expensive, then it was considered a luxury. It also seemed that people were very indoctrinated into eating meat.

They prepared a lot of meals in the kitchen and were especially busy when the Shawcrosses were entertaining. They would have the Davenports and Ardens into dinner. Peggy worked as the scullery maid. The cook was very brisk with everyone. "Oh Lord, oh mercy!" was one of her favourite sayings.

She complained that they should have a proper spit to turn the food for them above the log fire instead of the one they'd got, which meant them having to use their hands all the time. She would be saying "Oh Lord, oh mercy!" all the time while doing it.

The water they used for cooking had to be saved to do the washing up, and Peggy could not get used to the lighting. She was used to electricity, but this was just lanterns and though far from useless it was still not nearly good enough.

There was no glass at the window, just wooden shutters, and this would make it very steamy and smoky if they were kept shut, as they were if it was cold. They would have a log fire burning in the huge fireplace as it was needed for other things, and sometimes the cook would exclaim, "Oh open up the shutters!" Peggy could hardly see with it all, but opening them could make a cold wind rush in and any feathers that were being plucked would fly everywhere.

Yet when the shutters were open Peggy could both see and hear the market. What a noise! She noticed most the sound of cattle and she hated it; she thought of the animals all the time. She compared it with slavery.

But this was far from all that was going on. The marketplace was not just a place to buy and sell goods but the heart of the town. Public announcements would be made there, and criminals would be brought there and punished in the busiest part of it in front of their neighbours in order to humiliate them. For some it was a great source of entertainment.

She could also hear the cries of the traders and the bustle of the shoppers. People came from miles around to buy or sell their goods, and for some of the traders it was a long day, for they would start very early in the morning.

There was a wide range of things available, everything from beans to hats and, saucepans, but most of all Stockport was well known for its cheeses, which would sell everywhere, even as far as London.

"Leave the milk for the calf," Peggy would say as she continued to think about the animals. "We don't need it, and it's the calf's milk"

There was other food for sale, and the market would have strong smells of cooking. Sometimes things would be so nice and sometimes they would be absolutely dreadful, but Peggy knew she had to take the rough with the smooth. They once had a man tied up to a whipping stall for selling bad wine. They'd decided to give him a taste of his own medicine. They tried to make him drink the lot, and when he couldn't manage it they poured it all over him. Some of the crowd shouted, "Whip him, whip him!", but many more cried out telling them not to. They released him.

Another time an old woman, a fishmonger's wife, leapt back as a carthorse passed close enough to splatter her skirt. She shouted at the man responsible. How did she dare? Shortly after this another woman was brought forward; they said she had a malicious tongue that needed taming. They intended to put the scold bridle on her, a vicious instrument which consisted of an iron cage that was placed over the head and fastened. It had an extra metal plate with iron pins on the end that was inserted into the mouth. The poor wretch would therefore be unable to speak without a great deal of pain. It was used for scolding or swearing females, who were then led round the market as a punishment. This woman had eyes full of fear and pleading and on seeing Peggy with eyes full of pity, she cried out to her, "Have mercy upon me!"

Another person shouted out "Put her on the ducking stool!" This too was used to punish "scolds and unquiet women", as well as for fraudulent bakers or brewers of bad beer. A seat was fastened to the end of a long plank which was balanced so that it could be lowered into the water and raised. The woman was then put into it. The poor woman continued to look around her with pleading eyes and then one person said to Peggy, "What ducking stool? No one knows where there is one. Some people say it's in the pit at Cale Green, others say it's at Turnpole pit, Daw Bank, but no one's seen it"

The crowd continued to get excited but seemed to be focusing their attention on something else, which turned out to be the dungeons just a little down the hill. Peggy couldn't bear to go and see. She felt as though she wouldn't be able to take any more as there was still plenty of attention being paid to this other poor, poor woman.

One person said, "I'll pray for you!" but they were both pushed back by some official who shouted, "Keep away", and Mrs Shawcross then arrived and ordered Peggy back inside the house.

She cried herself to sleep that night wondering how much longer it would be before she could go back to Bowdon in 1959, and if she would ever get back there. She thought about how they would all be out looking for her, wondering where on earth could she be. It got darker and darker until she couldn't see at all, and then she fell fast asleep.

She woke up with a jolt. Was it morning? She felt it was, and yet at the same time it was still pitch black. She looked at the window to see that a little light was coming through, and then within minutes it was completely light again. She wondered how it could be so very dark and then quickly get so very light again.

"Whatever can the time be?" she exclaimed to herself as she jumped up. When she looked at the animals she noticed that her favourite dog, Jake, was no longer there; another very nice dog was in its place. As she looked closer she noticed that none of the animals were the same.

She went up to the kitchen to find that none of the people there were the same either. "Where is everyone?" she asked. They looked puzzled and then one said to the other "It's this war, its affecting a lot of people like this".

She started to try to help in the kitchen, but found they didn't want her. Then a butler came into the room, a different one, and said she was needed in the counting room. She couldn't understand it.

He took her there, and she found feather pens. A gentleman was sitting there.

"I hear you're very good at arithmetic" he told her. He gave her some maths to do and some money to add up, and she did it with no trouble at all.

"What's this war they're talking about?" she asked him.

"Well, the civil war of course" he told her. "We're being forced to take sides."

Now she realised she had gone forward in time.

"Whose side are you on?" she asked him.

"The King's."

The Parliamentarians were in control of Stockport, and were called to defend Manchester when the Royalists seized it in 1642. The Parliamentarians took a lot of property from the Royalists to fund their cause.

She heard about that when the Davenports arrived at the house for supper that night. It was from the maid Mary brought to wait on; she talked non-stop about it.

"Oh it was awful!" she said, obviously still very distressed about it. "They forced themselves into the house, the dog was barking away but that didn't stop them. "Out of the way!" they shouted. I cried out to Mrs Davenport that they were counting the silverware, but she told me to leave well alone or we'd be sharing a cell. Then they started on the books. I didn't know this, but John Shawcross has had 600 taken."

"What, John Shawcross from here?"

"Yes. Then they demanded the key to the chest. They were just shouting out orders, saying "What's behind here?" and so on, but Mrs Davenport had told me to leave them to it and so I did. After they had gone she said plenty. She said they would suck them dry. She said Parliament rewards those that denounce their King, and then they come and do this. She said no wonder the farmers had petitioned them to join the Parliamentarians, and yet at the same time she said it was time for her husband to enlist and fight for his King. "If only I was brave enough to show my wrath" she said.

"It seems that no one in Stockport knows which side to take."

"That's right, in fact they try not to take either, but it's coming to where we've got to choose. Mrs Davenport says her house is going to be a billet for either side, depending on who decides to barge in."

Then Mary talked about a Jane Done Bell who lived in Arden Hall. She was very much on the Parliamentarians' side, and she kept a bell to give the alarm should the Royalists arrive.

Now that it was 1662, Peggy was no longer expected to work in the kitchen or late. She only had to work in a room called the counting house, and she no longer had to sleep downstairs on the stone floor; she now had a proper bed to sleep in, in the room next to the counting house.

She could hear a commotion going on in the marketplace down below, and looked out of the window to see what it was all about. A big man had had a fit and he was accusing an old woman of having bewitched him. Although she looked very frightened, there were plenty of people very eager to defend her. They were saying such an idea was barbaric. One person shouted across to him that believing in witches was for gullible fools.

"What do you know about it?" shouted the man back, and then another man shouted, "String her up the wicked creature, she's the devil's hand!"

She was an ugly crone with a bent back, small and thin. Her hair was bedraggled, and the man got hold of her and started to shake her, saying, "Confess, confess! It was you that caused this fit."

Many of the crowd began to feel afraid, but one man shouted across loud and clear, "Let her be, she's not to blame!" Then another man came forward, a young man wearing a hat with a feather in it. "You stop that, just stop it" he firmly said, and the rest of the crowd cheered him and also told him to stop it. He let her go and she went on her way.

"Thank goodness for that" thought Peggy as she went back to her counting.

As she settled down for the night, she did so hope that she would be able to get back to 1959 in Bowdon. Maybe if every time she woke up she was a few years nearer to it, eventually she would get there.

But when she awoke this time, it was only next day. She went down to the basement to be with the animals and then went for a walk in the fields. She had started to go down the hill towards the river when a handsome young man rode passed on a horse. She knew who he would be, as Mary had talked about him. He would come from Dunham Hall to see Mrs Shawcross's young niece and when Peggy looked up at the window she saw her looking out. She didn't look very pleased to see him. Peggy continued on her way down to the river, but she hadn't been there long when he came riding up behind her.

"What do you want?" she asked him.

"Do you want a lift" he said.

"A lift to where?"

"A lift to Dunham Massey."

She jumped at this, and climbed on to the back of the horse. But what was she thinking of? She didn't have time to consider it, for soon they were riding away. They rode so fast that it didn't seem real, but she did hope that it would mean they were riding into the future. She knew she had strange powers and she remembered saying to Catherine, "If you yearn and yearn for a thing you get it". Then sure enough as they raced along faster than a train she could see modern buildings flashing by. She even at one point recognized the Devisdale and a Victorian mansion on it. There was a big garden party going on and a notice up saying "The Vegetarian Society". She wanted to stop and join them. Everyone at the party was in modern clothes; in fact more than that, they seemed to be ahead of the fashions. He rode his horse round and round trying to find it for her, but he said he couldn't see it. Then he slowed down and they were going back to the 1600s again.

"Keep riding fast!" she told him, but she didn't tell him why. They galloped along at great speed again and when they came to Dunham Park she felt full of hope, for she saw someone she recognized – Lord Stamford, the one who would blow his whistle if they were up a tree. But then as they slowed down he quickly disappeared, and they were quickly back in 1662.

"Come inside" said the young man as they drew up outside a big mansion. A grand lady was just leaving in a horse and carriage, but she didn't seem to notice them. They went into a grand hall and then into another very big room full of grand furniture.

"Let's go upstairs and I'll get you something to eat" he told her. They went into a big dining room and he ordered something for them both.

"Who will they think I am?" she asked.

"I don't know and I don't care."

"But you are a gentleman and I'm a servant girl. Will that be accepted?"

"No. And I don't care."

But she did care, and when another fine lady came into the room and started looking at her disapprovingly Peggy ran out and down the servants' staircase. The young man ran after her, and they jumped straight into a horse and carriage. There was someone to take them, and they were away.

"Let's go past Bowdon Church" she said. He shouted at the driver, "Bowdon Church!"

"Now let's go down the path that will be one day named after Lord Stamford and be called Stamford Road" she said, and he immediately told the driver to so. She wished that all men were like this and just did as they were told. She looked at the wooden houses dotted about and built on either side of it. If only she could get back to the one in 1959 where she had lived with her grandmother.

"Tell the driver to ride faster, so we ride into the future" she said. He laughed and told her they weren't as clever as that; he didn't seem aware that they had already travelled into the future. They rode on, and rode faster until they reached the 1870s. She recognised Altrincham Hospital, even though some of it had been demolished in 1911. She knew that it had previously been Lloyds Fever Hospital, transferred from Lloyd Street in Altrincham in 1872 to become Altrincham General Hospital. She recognised from a picture its first matron, a Mrs Tatham, who was just leaving the hospital and was standing on the front steps. She had been given residence there with her husband. She had read that Mrs Tatham was not a trained nurse and it had been said at a meeting that in future the matron must always be trained; by the 1950s a lot of people thought that was taken for granted. There had been trouble about her keeping pigs in the hospital yard, in fact she was told she couldn't do it any more, and people many years later thought that this too should go without saying. Yet they wanted to keep her. She had daughters and had refused to stay there unless accommodation was provided which made it possible for them to come and stay with her.

The young man slowed down, and as they approached Stockport she suddenly heard the noise of a battle. "Oh no!" she thought, "It's the civil war." Maybe they should have stayed in Bowdon. But he wouldn't turn back.

"Oh please go back!" she pleaded with him, but then she realised that nothing had been as bad as she thought. They stopped and hid behind a very big bush, almost a tree. Prince Rupert had arrived with an army of 10,000 men to cross the River Mersey via the Lancashire Bridge. The Parliamentarians in Stockport only had 3,000 men, yet they still didn't give in immediately. It took them a little while before they decided to withdraw their troops and let Prince Rupert in. Now the people of Stockport were watching a procession of richly-attired Royalists coming over the bridge.

Peggy soon decided it would be safe for them to return to Staircase House, and she was glad to be back. No one asked her where she'd been. No one seemed bothered either about Prince Rupert. Although he didn't stay long he did leave a few dragoons to hold the bridge. They were right not to be bothered, for that didn't last for long, and shortly after he was thoroughly defeated.

Peggy soon began to feel unsettled again. She started to yearn to be back in Bowdon 1959, even though she was no longer sleeping on cushions on a stone floor but in a comfortable bed.

One night as she lay dozing she felt that something was not right. It was getting darker and darker, until she was sound asleep. Suddenly she awoke; now everything seemed all wrong and she was in pitch black darkness. The lanterns had all gone, and when she got up she found herself fumbling about in the dark.

Slowly a light started to show from the window, so she got back into bed and fell back to sleep. She began to dream. She was back again on the back of a horse and saying, "Faster, faster, ride into the future!"

She suddenly awoke, sat up and wondered if it was a dream or if it was her strange powers, for she could indeed hear horses galloping past; they were going very fast and she felt certain she was going into the future. She tried to call out to them, "Faster, faster!" to find that there was now glass in the window, so she banged on it instead and shouted, "Ride on, ride on, ride into the future!" Dozens of them did so, going faster than a train.

But she could take no more of it. She was exhausted, so she went back to bed and this time she slept peacefully until the next evening. When she awoke everything was quiet and peaceful. When she looked out of the window she could see two horses quietly grazing in the grass; the wild dreams had all gone.

She went into the next room to find herself in a dining room full of Victorians having a dinner party. They ignored her as though she was invisible, but as she stood there she found the conversation very interesting. It was about the Royal family. First they were talking about young Prince Edward; he had been to a music hall and at the end he had gone to the back of the stage and asked to see one of the girls he had seen dancing on the stage.

"Oh, your Royal Highness!" she had said when she first came face to face with him and started to curtsey, but he brought out a bunch of flowers he had hidden behind his back and said, "Call me Bertie" and gave them to her. His parents, Queen Victoria and Prince Albert, were furious when it got back to them and then the people around the dinner table started to talk about another scandal. A man at the palace had been caught cheating at cards. It was considered very serious. They had tried to hush it up, as they didn't want it known that such people went to the palace, but it was without success. There was a woman in their circle who knew about it, and she had a mouth so big that she was known as "Mrs Blab". But it wasn't all gossip. They made mention of someone they knew, a sea captain, and Peggy noted with interest how they were saying that he captained a ship that transported slaves. They clearly considered this to be a respected profession.

It reminded her of 1959 and some of the live exports on passenger boats she had seen down at the docks at Dover. It was dreadfully cruel. They were crammed up together like slaves, very frightened, and the journey could be so bad they could die on it.

She went back to her room and wondered what her duties would be now that they were in the Victorian period. Yet it seemed that she was invisible and no one knew she was there. She still felt quite tired, so she got back into bed and drifted off into another sleep.

When she awoke she found herself in a completely different room and in a completely different bed, yet she knew it was Staircase House and she could still see the market from the window. There was a road outside with cars in it, all black. She must have got back almost to 1959.

She also soon realised she was no longer invisible; a middle-aged woman came into the room, and then another, carrying a tray with her breakfast on it. They seemed to think she was a friend of one of their daughters. They were listening to the radio. It was a big old-fashioned one, and Sir Winston Churchill was talking on it. Germany had just signed a treaty with Russia and although the two women looked very glum they looked a lot more optimistic after listening to him. Churchill had said with very great confidence: "Nothing to worry about, we're going to win this war".

They looked at one another with great enthusiasm and said, "That's right, we're going to win". No one would have imagined that only minutes before they had been discussing how they would manage now that the Germans were certain to invade.

At that moment the sirens went off. Peggy was afraid she was going to be killed in an air raid and that she would never get back to Bowdon 1959. "Calm down" said one of the women to her. "We'll get to the air raid shelter in plenty of time."

"Where are they?" she cried out. They told her. They all ran down the hill to Chestergate and into the shelter. It wasn't peaceful in there, not only because of the fighting that was going on in the air above them but a fight raging between two men in the tunnels and then in one of the rooms which ran under the ground as far back as St. Peter's Church. They were both very drunk. The officials got hold of them one at a time and threw them into a cell.

Shortly after that, the sirens went off to say that it was safe, so they all came out again and she went off back up the hill and into Staircase House. Then in what seemed like no time at all the sirens started going off again. This time there was a bit of a panic all round, as another middle-aged woman appeared and shouted "They're coming back!"

They started to rush down the staircase together faster, faster. They were both really panicking now, falling over one another, as it looked as though they were going to be too late. They could see that there were some planes above them with swastikas on them. Then the anti-aircraft guns began and the noise was deafening.

Peggy fell. She began to roll down and down, and she called out to herself, "Roll on, roll on, roll into the future!" She was afraid. Where was it all going to end? The staircase seemed to be going on for ever. Then suddenly it all came to a standstill and everything was quiet. She had reached the bottom.

She opened her eyes to find Jessica standing above her.

"You fainted" she said. A woman was sweeping up the glass and all the mess she had made when going over. She was back in Stockport Market, 1959. They told her that she had only been out for a minute.

They walked up together to Staircase House to find that it was now a museum. Peggy saw the scold bridle on show, but she noticed at the same time that they had no record of it ever being used. She clung on to the hope that this meant that it never had been, and that some mercy had been shown for the woman she had seen.

She saw the lanterns hanging up, with an electric light on as well, not very bright and a notice up saying they had to have them as no one would be able to see properly without them. She saw some of the clothes they had worn in those days on display, but noticed that there were only those of the ladies; the maids' clothes were far too poorly made to last.

She then went to have a look at the dungeons that she had heard everyone talking about, although she had never been to see them herself when she had been there at the time when they had been in use.

They went into St Mary's Church and Peggy was able to read about something else that had happened at about the time she had been there. The water in the River Mersey had come up so high that it had reached the top of Lancashire Bridge, the one Prince Rupert had used, a bridge that can still be seen in Warren Street in Stockport Town Centre. She read what a farmer called John Ryle had written about it. He had been there at the time, and said it had been impossible to ride across. He had wanted to get to School House, but several people had told him he should not even try to ride over the Bearholes unless he could swim. He rode up Hillgate instead and through Edgeley to get home. The School House he talked about was the old Grammar School which was on Great Underbank.

She also read that 'Madde Marye', the first victim for whom the plague bell tolled in 1605, was buried in the churchyard there and also that Judge Bradshawe, said to have been born in Marple in 1602, was baptised in St Mary's Church. He gained renown when, as President of the High Court of Justice, he signed the death warrant of King Charles I and against the entry of his baptism in the parish register is written anonymously 'traitor'. He died in 1659, the year before Charles II was restored to the throne. In 1661 the judge's body was exhumed, hung in chains and decapitated, his head being displayed on a pike at Westminster Hall and the rest of his body thrown into a pit with Cromwell's, which had received the same treatment.

She went to Dunham Hall to see who the man would be who had taken her there on a horse. She could find no record, but going by portraits of some of the Booths, clearly he had been one of them, and clearly they had known who he was when she'd been there with him in 1662. He also seemed to know all about the civil war.

Chapter Five

CATHERINE IN THE 20TH CENTURY

After all this Peggy found it very difficult to adjust to modern times. Yet life did go on, and it was back to school every day. There had been a big row about something. They had all been told to write an essay on "their day" and Jessica had written that she got up every morning at eight to do her homework. She had forgotten that this was forbidden. She wasn't all that interested, but the head teacher was straight on the phone to her grandmother about it, saying that homework must only be done in the evening with the television off and sitting up at a table. It was not to be rushed through in the mornings.

In class that day one of the girls, Carol, hissed something about it into Peggy's ear.

"Hush!" said Peggy "She's got ears like a hawk."

The teacher, Miss Hodgson, called across the classroom to her "Peggy, it's eyes like a hawk, you don't have ears like a hawk!"

Peggy hissed back, but much quieter this time to Carol, "What was that I was just telling you? She's got ears like a hawk."

Next there was trouble about the school hat. Oh, the endless trouble the schools would go to to get the girls to wear their hats! It was as though it had become a challenge on both sides. Jessica had lost hers.

"Where's the money coming from for you to get another?" A teacher asked her.

"Oh that'll be Dad, he'll pay for that."

"I don't see why he should."

"No, nor do I, but he will do, honestly, it will be all right."

She pretended to refuse to get the point that she shouldn't be so careless as to lose it in the first place and that her father shouldn't have to pay for it if she did. She continued to wind up the teacher by saying, "Honestly, I'll soon have another one, Dad'll see to that".

They didn't hate school, but they found it very boring being told all the time that they should be thinking about their future and what they would be doing for a living for the rest of their lives Couldn't it wait? Couldn't they just live for the day and go through life like this? And then the arithmetic teacher, Mrs Theobald, gave them a shock. Some girls had got 100% in a test, and the teacher knew very well how they'd done that – they'd cheated. She got one of them up at the blackboard and made her work out a sum. The girl did it, but with great difficulty and not without help from Mrs Theobald. She was furious. She bawled, "You got 100% in your test and you can't work that out? Just who do you think you're cheating? No one else but yourself! Did you really think I would believe it, that I wouldn't know how you got it? After you have left school your employers will be laughing. They'll be saying, "We don't have to pay her properly, she can't do arithmetic. She cheated at school and now we can cheat her".

Then she came out with something horrendous. She started talking about the Inland Revenue. "And they too will be laughing, they'll be saying, "We can make her pay as much tax as we like, she can't do arithmetic.""

The class couldn't accept that. They believed that the Inland Revenue were all middle-aged men in suits who would of course be nothing but scrupulous, and their only interest would be to collect the taxes which were due. How could Mrs Theobald suggest such a thing? But next day there was something in the newspapers about one of them fiddling the taxes for himself, not declaring everything, and one wondered if Mrs Theobald knew something about it.

A fire inspector came up to show them how a fire extinguisher worked and they all went out into the playground to practise using one. They found it very amusing. They chased one another with them and made jokes about having to run out in an emergency with one.

Once back inside in the hall, they settled down to have a talk on the subject. The first thing the inspector told them was how typical it was to think that fire was a big joke. He went on to talk about other things, mainly how to get out if there was a fire, knowing where the emergency doors were. He emphasized how they were to try not to panic. Often people get killed in fires unnecessarily, because they have done something like jump out of a high window. One man had run out of Woolworths in Manchester straight in front of a car.

Then a voice at the back of the room called out, "Tell us more about the Great Fire of London."

Everyone turned round to look. Catherine was standing there. When had she come in? She was wearing modern clothes, although they were quite shabby. She had on a grey full skirt and a dark purple jumper. It certainly wasn't school uniform.

The teacher in charge didn't quite know what to say. "She's not one of us", she told him, and yet she was pleased that someone was taking an interest. He told the pupils that after the Great Fire of London, new rules were made to prevent such a disaster happening again. Buildings were to be made from brick and stone rather than wood. Houses could only be two storeys high in the back streets or four storeys in the main ones, and were to be built further apart. New regulations were introduced about firefighting. New equipment was bought. Each area of London had to have a certain number of buckets, ladders and hand squirts. Later on, the first horse-drawn fire engines appeared. Towns all over Britain started making certain they had the same precautions.

"What happened to Ginger?" asked Catherine.

"Who's Ginger?" said the fire inspector.

"A young lad who worked in a baker's in Pudding Lane" said Catherine. He didn't know, but the teacher, Mrs Moss, had more idea about what might have happened and for the first time Catherine, Jessica and Peggy found out that this was where the fire had first started, in the baker's where he worked. The teacher was not aware that there was any apprentice there called Ginger, but she did know that the assistant, Bessie, had been killed in the fire. All three girls gasped in horror when they heard that, and the rest of the class thought it seemed they had personally known the woman.

The teacher went on, "A lot of it we can only guess, I've seen no record of any apprentice being killed in a baker's shop and there would have been if he had."

"What happened to those who weren't killed?" asked Catherine, extremely relieved that at least Ginger hadn't been.

"A lot of them camped out by the river like refugees, I'm afraid" said Mrs Moss, seeing Catherine was finding it upsetting.

"How do you mean?"

"Well, there was a lot of work to be done and many people said London would never be the same again. 400 streets, over 13,000 houses and 87 churches were destroyed."

"Would it be safe to go there now?" asked Catherine. Everyone laughed.

"Well, Charles the Second had dreams of wide streets, great parks and no overcrowding. Great architects like Sir Christopher Wren began to plan. London would become a beautiful city. But it turned out not to be realistic. There was neither the time nor the money, even though lots of people were sending contributions. Tradesmen needed to get their businesses up and running again and the cheapest way of doing this was for everyone to build their own property in the same place as it was before."

"I would love to see London as it is today" said Catherine.

"I'll make certain you go" said another teacher. That was a rash promise for her to make, but she was a very kind person. She had promised too much in front of the headmistress, yet she had wanted so much to encourage this young girl, and a girl that looked so poor. Who was she in any case?

* * * * *

"Oh, do please say she's your niece" said Jessica to her grandmother. "Only she can't go to London if you don't, we're all going on a day trip there."

"If she was my niece then it should be me that's paying for it, not the teacher at school."

Catherine did go to London. Mrs Newton paid for it and no one asked too closely who she was. The first thing she enjoyed was when she went into a restaurant for lunch. Two of them were vegetarians and had given notice before to say they were coming, then after they arrived two more said they were also vegetarians, so something was prepared for them, and then another girl decided to join them. The head of the kitchen came out to say could they please close it on that, as he couldn't have people keep changing their minds, when the manager started coming down the stairs. He took an interest in what was going on and stopped to have a word with the one of the teachers, who was about 35. The girls were most interested and amused by what followed. He was trying to chat her up. He was saying that he would shortly be in her part of the world and maybe they could have lunch together.

They had thought of her as so old before. In those days a woman would be on the shelf if she wasn't married by the time she was 28. However, this teacher told him no. Maybe what surprised the girls most was that she didn't seem to be all that surprised. It was almost as though she was used to it. They went home giggling to tell all their friends.

Catherine loved seeing the Tower of London as a tourist attraction and no longer a place to fear. It also fascinated her that there was a pub called the Royal Oak, for she knew it was named after King Charles the Second, who had hidden up an oak tree after having lost the battle of Worcester. She saw St Paul's Cathedral, yet most of all she loved the coffee houses. She knew that coffee had first been brought over from the Middle East, and that it was when she was just a baby in 1652 that they had first started opening coffee houses in London. They soon spread and became places to go to to gossip. She liked that part of it and would sometimes go with her mother, but she found that they could also be very boring places where people would discuss politics or have business meetings.

But for today she loved the food, and they all knew it was not to be taken for granted. Jessica and Peggy remembered rationing after the war and how their mother would never let them forget it. Although at times Catherine had eaten like a queen, at others she'd been sleeping rough and had been quite hungry.

She knew quite a bit about the history of food in the 17th century. Gardens began to be cultivated and various fruits started coming over from Europe. But Catherine remembered most of all the good fire in the hall, sitting there with her mother, eating bread pudding and sauce, good mustard, cheese and nuts, and sometimes jolly carols to listen to.

On top of this, carpets began to take the place of rushes and mats. Weavers soon learned how to imitate the carpets that came from Turkey. Chairs were cushioned and feather beds took the place of straw ones, yet Catherine felt there was nothing more comfortable than the one she slept in at Willow Tree Cottage.

She continued to marvel at the way Catholics and Protestants got on together without fighting or fear of one another. She thought it was wonderful the way a Protestant could go into a Catholic church to pray if he wanted to. She thought it was great the way England and Scotland were joined together, although they did have separate parliaments, and if anyone said this wasn't good enough and wanted to be more separate, they would protest about it, but peacefully.

She couldn't understand why some people insisted on calling the monarch Queen Elizabeth the Second of England and Scotland, because she was Queen Elizabeth the First of Scotland; Queen Elizabeth I was only Queen of England and Wales. In fact when she first became Queen, some Scots were taking signs that bore this title off letterboxes.

A march went by. "What's that?" Catherine asked.

"Oh that's a new campaign that's just started up called the

Campaign for Nuclear Disarmament. They want everyone to get rid of all of their weapons so that we can stop all this killing one another."

Catherine made no comment, although it sounded like a splendid idea to her.

"It's always very peaceful, is it?"

"Oh no."

"What do you mean?" someone else in the group asked, because as far as she knew it always was.

"I mean you can't turn on the television without hearing about some disruption that's going on. The news is always the same, the CND will be having a meeting with the police about how out of hand their last demonstration got."

"But that's only because people never like anything that's new" said the teacher. "And the CND hasn't been going very long."

"Well they've got plenty of complaints about the police being heavy handed."

"The police are only a cross-section of people and some of them will be out of order."

"You hear so many yarns you don't know which to believe" said another teacher.

People were also saying that a lot of CND members were very scruffy and that they were doing themselves down by being like that, but the CND defended themselves by saying they'd just been on a long march so they couldn't be expected to be always looking smart.

"If we get rid of our weapons the enemy won't get rid of theirs, and we'll only find out when they're marching in on us and we've got no army" said Jessica.

"Of course they would if they could" said someone on the march who was giving out leaflets about it. 'We'll have means of inspecting them and what's going on."

"When?" someone else asked.

"Not in the near future." The CND had certainly got people talking about it.

But most of all Catherine went to see the monument which marked the spot where the great fire had first started. Now she knew it was the same spot, she would go to meet Ginger. If only he would appear now.

She looked longingly at Peggy, as she knew what strange powers she had, but Peggy didn't seem to be able to do anything. How different the place looked now. It was unrecognisable, full of traffic and high-rise buildings. They went down to the Thames, but the route was completely different. They walked along the side of the river until it was time to go. They had to get a taxi, they were so late. They remarked to the taxi driver how very different everything was.

"You can say that again" he told them. "And that's not only in London. You don't know where you are the way they're pulling buildings down and putting new ones up all the time. One day I had a passenger in the back and I thought, 'if when I turn round this corner there isn't a church on the left, I'm going to say to my passenger, I've got a confession to make, I'm lost'. I turned the corner and there was a church on the left. I breathed a sigh of relief."

Back in Bowdon next day, they went back to the usual routine. The journey back on the coach was every bit as exciting to Catherine as the one down. She'd never been so fast, she'd never been so high before. She was upstairs, and now she felt she would like to ride a bicycle.

When they came back they were all very tired. Their grandmother had a friend visiting called John Chesters, and he knew her son, the girls' father. He was from the university. It was most interesting what he was talking about; it was about a man who lived opposite where he worked in Dover Street, at Manchester University, and he was under sentence of death. It wasn't particularly interesting to Catherine; most people she knew had seen an execution.

"Are you going to go and watch it?" she asked.

"I'd love to" he laughed, thinking it was a joke and he was joining in with it, and yet, at the same time, he hated murderers. "Are you?"

"Oh no!" she exclaimed "I've never had a real good look, it's horrible, and it's absolutely hateful when all the crowd start shouting 'Do it slowly, do it slowly!'"

Jessica and Peggy immediately realised that she did not know that those days had gone. They were scared she was going to give the game away, so Peggy hurriedly said "How could you talk like that when all public executions were stopped nearly a hundred years ago?"

"Well" said Catherine. "If they can't go and see an execution they go to look at people in the lunatic asylum. They'll have that for entertainment instead."

"There's a bit of that going on these days" said Mrs Newton, thinking about the woman who lived next to the post office in Bowdon and how some people would wind her up to get a good show going.

Then she had more to say about executions. "You still get people these days who will hang around outside the prison and wait to see the notice put out on the door to say that the execution has taken place" she said. She had lived in London and sometimes gone past the prison on a bus when on her way to work.

"But some of those people are protesting about it, trying to get the death sentence abolished" said Jessica. She was going by what she had seen on the news at the time about Ruth Ellis, the last woman to be hanged in Britain. An angry crowd had charged forward when the notice went up to say they had done it, and yet at that time, just before nine o'clock that morning, they couldn't possibly have thought they were going to be able to stop it. They could only have been angry that someone could be hanged.

"What's really wrong is that it's irreversible. They have sometimes hanged the wrong man" said Mrs Newton.

"Well this man who lives opposite where I work has done it all right, and his wife is a little lady. She picked up a grid in the road and chucked it at the police"

"But it doesn't deserve a death sentence."

"It's not his wife that's under sentence of death."

However the condemned man was shortly not just reprieved but exonerated. The police were determined to get him after that. It was always in the papers that he had been run in for something. It seemed they just sat and waited, and they wouldn't have to wait for long. He stole his sister's television. By now quite a few more people were getting TVs but they were still something of a luxury. It never crossed the woman's mind her brother had taken it until the police went round to his house to get it back.

They talked about the "Let him have it" case, when PC Simon Miles, a police officer aged only 41, had had a bullet put through his brain while making certain that someone didn't have their belongings taken. They couldn't hang the lad who pulled the trigger, Christopher Craig, as he was only 16, but they did hang Derek Bentley, aged 19, who was with him at the time. They said he had shouted to Craig "Let him have it", and that meant it was murder. Bentley denied he had said it.

"Well both of them had an appalling record of theft" said John Chesters.

"That doesn't deserve a death sentence."

Yet it was enough to stop John Chesters feeling any sympathy. "Get him out of the way while we have the chance" he said.

Bentley had been hanged in 1953 and the case was still fresh in a lot of people's minds. Bentley and Craig had been on a roof top and were both aware of what was going on beneath them. Police were climbing up to get them. They told them to come down and Craig had bawled at them "If you want me then fucking come up and get me." And so they did. When they got there Craig shot PC Miles.

Some people said the police had made it up that Bentley had said "Let him have it" because they were determined to get someone's blood for it, and they knew they couldn't get Craig as he was under age.

John Chesters sat discussing it, still unsympathetic, and then he said, "Could you imagine what it was like for them? A colleague of theirs, someone they worked with and saw every day, had been murdered, and on the same day, only a couple of hours later, they had the men down in the police station who had done it. It's a wonder that they didn't beat them up."

"They probably did" said Jessica.

Mrs Newton told him, "Yes, I can well imagine the hate I would have in my heart if I had been in the shoes of the police, I might have done the same myself, but that doesn't mean it's right."

"Well it won't be me that stops you."

"Doesn't it show a whole team can go wrong?"

"Well, it's been nowhere near proved that these three police officers did conspire to say that, it's only what some people say."

"And they say it because it looks so very like it, and it would be very easy for them to do it. They would know what the law is, what to make up in order to get him convicted, and it's not a long, complicated lie they planned to tell, it was something short and simple."

"Yes. It would be something they would easily be able to say in court when being cross-examined."

"Well we've got to stop the death sentence" said Mrs Newton. "They might hang the wrong man."

"Perhaps one day they will find a way of testing people to tell for sure if they were at the scene of a crime" said John. "They're talking about something that they will call DNA."

"That would only prove he did it. It won't tell you whether it was in self-defence or whether the balance of his mind was disturbed. In fact there are a lot of things it won't tell you."

The women went on and on about this until Peggy came out with, "Do you know that one of those police officers was called Fairy? What a name!"

In fact his name was Fairfax and his colleagues had called him Fairy for short, and it was no joke. They were still very upset at what had happened and making statements about it, yet a girl in their school had a father with the same name and his family would call him Fairy for short.

As regards getting the wrong man convicted for murder, it was often a case of "Thank goodness we didn't hang that man". Yet it stands to reason. The evidence remains if they still have him. It was also noted that in America, when a man was on death row, it would often emerge as the years went by that he was innocent.

Jessica and Peggy listened to all this, having always accepted that if someone kills someone they shouldn't be allowed to live themselves. She had been brought up to believe it. It was something that went unsaid. They went to bed that night very thoughtful.

Chapter Six

JESSICA IN HOSPITAL

The next evening Peter Brown arrived again to take Jessica out. He had a mate, David, with him, also on a motorbike. He had come for Peggy, but she refused to go, so only the three to them went, Jessica on the back of Peter's bike.

They rode down Grange Road, going for a run by the River Bollin. She saw the building again and was told it was a nursing home and they employed young girls there and paid them a pound a day. It wasn't only that the money sounded good, but the place looked nice. It was an old Victorian building in the middle of a field.

Jessica clung on to Peter more closely as he rode on, and when they arrived at the riverside she said, "Let me have a ride on my own". David came with her and they said goodbye to Peter, leaving him with some more of his mates as they rode off side by side.

By now she'd had several goes at learning to ride a motorbike, but this time everything had suddenly come together and she found she was doing it fluently. She kicked the starter and the engine roared happily to life. Then she twisted the throttle and felt the power surge under her. She let in the clutch and lifted her feet from the ground, and with no effort of her own it carried her forward. She leaned on the handlebars, opened the throttle, and the machine surged along the road. Flying couldn't have been any better.

She made her way towards South Downs Road, and David overtook her, so she picked up speed and overtook him. He shouted "Well done!" as she passed. The sun shone and the air rushed past her. She felt as though people were looking round at her, admiring her with the throb of the engine and the promise of speed and power.

She did a U-turn at the end of the road, sped back and then turned right into Marlborough Road. David followed and overtook her just by the boys' grammar school, but she soon overtook him again.

She was not quite so carried away when riding the bike through Hale. It moved obediently on, and she slowed down as she wove in and out of traffic. She found she still had perfect control, but once she was away from the houses and shops she opened up the throttle again and felt the power surge under her. She went along Langham Road, the sun shining on her back and the wind in her face. It was magnificent, unbelievable. Sometimes she lost David for a while, but he always turned up again.

She turned into Grange Road and rode towards the Bollin. She was taking it back to Peter, and now she had David closely behind. A horse in a field galloped away at the roar of her passing. She had to slow down again as she zigzagged between potholes and past the nursing home run by the nuns. She would soon be on a much wider path again, that is if she knew where she was, and she'd be able to open the throttle again.

She found the road here was a good bit narrower than she thought it was. It wasn't as long as she thought, and full of trees…

The next thing she remembered was waking up in hospital. Her father was by her side.

"You've had an accident" he very gently told her.

"What happened?"

"No one's certain. Don't think about it for now."

She didn't. She slowly recovered over the next few days, sitting most of the time by the side of her bed in an armchair, although she did sometimes go into the day room. Then the police came to see her. By now she knew that they didn't know what had happened and she had also found out from someone she'd met in the dayroom that she could say she couldn't remember any of it. This man had been in an accident himself and knew that this can sometimes happen.

Jessica wasn't going to say to the police that she had been riding a motorbike; she was under age and hadn't got any sort of a licence. She had been seen going off with Peter Brown only an hour or two before, but he was safe, he had an alibi as to where he was at the time of the accident. It seemed David had managed to get an ambulance very quickly, and then get both motor bikes out of sight.

The police enquiries didn't go on for very long. She came out of hospital shortly after and went home to her grandmother's. Her father had to be taken straight back to prison. She had been put off bikes and she never wanted to learn to drive a car either. She was off the roads for life.

During her rehabilitation she also started thinking more seriously about applying to be a nurse. She thought about the big house, the residential home for old people run by nuns. When she felt better she knocked on the door and asked if there were any jobs going. She felt apprehensive, as she had friends who had been taught at school by nuns and they had told her that some of them can have some mighty peculiar ideas. But as she sat there being interviewed, she began to feel quite relaxed. There was certainly nothing strange about the Mother Superior. She got a Saturday job straight away. You could get them easily in 1959. She would be earning a pound a day.

She felt nervous on her first Saturday, although she was usually full of life and cheek. The Mother Superior introduced her to another girl called Carol, not much older than she was. She was given an overall to wear and three of them immediately got down to work. Another nun, Sister St Clare, a trained nurse, came with them. The work was mainly getting old people out of bed and washed, then giving them a cup of tea while they waited for breakfast. Jessica was told it would be better to give them water, if she could, to stop them getting dehydrated, but the trouble was that often they would drink their cup of tea but they wouldn't drink the water.

It was Jessica's job to push the tea trolley round, but she was very slow, being new to the job. And the residents wouldn't answer when she asked, "Who wants a cup of tea?" She was told it would be better to ask them to put their hand up if they wanted one. It's not just old people who won't answer. One of the other girls working there had been a waitress in other places and said she'd had the same problem.

That was the easy part of the day. When it came to lifting she found she wasn't used to it. Whoever was lifting with her would be taking all the weight. She was told to try to put it on to her legs instead of her back as she might hurt it otherwise, but it became obvious she needed practice.

It saddened Jessica the way the residents were all talking about going home, because she felt certain they never would. Yet they all seemed to believe they were in there temporarily. Someone told her that their relatives would never get them in there in the first place if they didn't tell them they were going home again.

"Well, they could use force, but who wants that?" said the Mother Superior. Jessica didn't. She could never imagine herself doing such a thing to either of her parents. "Honour thy father and mother" she said. Jessica, usually without a care in the world, was now beginning to think seriously about something.

After morning break she went round giving out jugs of water with glasses to put on the lockers. She went into one room and found the woman lying there dead. She went to get Sister St Clare. "Come and have a look at this!" she said. She was surprised that she didn't feel more shaken than she did, for she had never seen anyone dead before.

Carol asked her "Are you all right?"

"Oh yes, I'm all right, but I think it's a shame that she came in here and never went out again."

"But she did" said Sister St Clare. "Her relatives would come sometimes and take her home for as long as a week."

When visitors came she sat with them in the day room having another break. One of them told her how her old mother would talk all the time about going home, and then they had a phone call in the middle of the night to say that she had had a fall and was now in hospital. They all went rushing down to see her, and when she started talking about going home, which she very soon did, it was the care home she was talking about. She now considered it to be her home. They were very soon able to get her out and back there and she had considered it to be home ever since.

There were no rules about visiting hours – it was a home, not an institution – but they did say at what times they would prefer visitors not to come. Sometimes they would have to put their foot down if they had someone very ill or even dying. People who are on their way out don't want to be in a place where there's a lot of coming and going, so often when this sort of thing happened they would put them into a room on their own. They did plan for everyone to have a room of their own eventually, and also to give the relatives a place where they could go and make themselves a cup of tea. Old people like to be with family, and having them free to drop in and have a cup of tea whenever they wanted would make the residents feel at home.

When she was back again and at work, the Mother Superior, also a trained nurse, came to join them, and was feeding one of the residents. They talked. Jessica said, "Isn't it good the way it doesn't matter if you are a Catholic or a Protestant here."

"Indeed it is."

"Well I know a school where they will favour a child if she's a Roman Catholic."

Jessica wished she hadn't said it, for clearly the Mother Superior didn't like it and nor did Sister St Clare. Yet she knew more about that school; they were absurdly modest. Once when they had to put words into sentences, the word had been "bare" and they put things like, "I got into the bath bare." There was a big row about it. They were supposed to only talk about things like bare feet. One mother was so disgusted with the nuns that she took her child away from the school. She didn't want her being educated like that. She wrote to the nuns and said, "Are we allowed to talk about the Garden of Eden? Because there was plenty of nudity in there."

Jessica knew there was plenty of nudity in the nursing home; in fact there was no modesty whatsoever apart from putting screens up when it came to washing and getting dressed.

One thing horrified her. A patient had been brought in with a dreadful bedsore on her heel. It was gangrenous and stank, and it was going to take a lot of time and dressings to get it put right. The woman was bedridden, or at least chair-ridden, as she spent a lot of time out of bed sitting beside it. Jessica couldn't see how she'd ever be able to walk again with a heel like that, even if nothing else was stopping her.

She went down for several more Saturdays, but she was beginning to find it exhausting. She would have her dinner there and feel too tired sometimes to pick up her knife and fork to eat. Yet she very much appreciated the pound she was paid for it; it changed her week completely with what she could buy with it.

Then a doctor arrived who wanted tests doing on some of them to see if they were confused at all, and if so how much. They were amazed at some of the answers they got. For example, Jessica was not the only one to say that Mrs Jacobs was perfectly with it, yet some of the answers she was giving were astounding. To start off with, Jessica was embarrassed; it was so obvious it was suggesting she was a dippy old woman. She went up to her, laughing, to cover her embarrassment, and said, "Now these are just routine, we ask everyone."

The first question was, who is the Queen of England? Mrs Jacobs laughed too as though to cover up embarrassment and said, "Well, Queen Victoria of course."

They worked out that she would have been 25 when Queen Victoria died. It did show that you can believe two things at the same time, because when Mrs Jacobs was reading the newspapers later she showed that she knew Elizabeth was Queen. It reminded Jessica of the time she was saying that New York was the capital of the United States and yet when someone said to her that it wasn't, it was Washington, she was able to say that she already knew that.

It may seem strange that on top of this the carers were saying that these residents weren't confused at all, although they were. They couldn't accept it when they could so very easily hold a sensible conversation with them and could give an opinion on something. Does it matter who the Queen of England is? The Mother Superior said she'd never known someone to be stopped from going home because they didn't know that.

One woman got it right when she was asked who the Prime Minister was during the war, but then added, "He was very badly treated after".

Jessica had been told she was to write down precisely what they had said, so she did. The doctor in the office asked her if she knew what the woman had meant, but she didn't. He explained that after taking us through the war, Churchill had lost the next election. He asked her if she had thought it was because she was a dippy old woman that she had said this, and Jessica admitted that she had. It made them laugh that the test was supposed to be for the residents, yet in this case a carer hadn't passed the test.

Some time later a couple of the nurses started talking about the results of an election. It was frightening that the Neo-Nazis in Germany had got so many votes. Everyone thought that those days had gone and the war had smashed fascism. One of the residents who had done so badly in the test interrupted them with, "It can't make your blood run cold like it did mine, I lived through it all, don't say this is starting up again." It showed how with it she was.

It wasn't until later that they discovered that fascism wasn't confined to Germany but spreading all over Europe, and there would be an ongoing fight against fascism and people who still admired Hitler.

A girl called Maria came to work there. She was 23 but behaved as though she was 13, and seemed very shy and inexperienced. She lived in, so she had a small cubicle and a few belongings, and had all her meals at the home. She didn't do a lot of the nursing and was used to children. She came from a big family with many small brothers and sisters, and as soon as she'd left school she had got a job working with children.

"Why don't you train to be a nursery nurse?" people asked her. She didn't want to, although she had done plenty of correspondence courses. She had been turned out of where she'd been living before because she'd been ill and the family she'd been working for didn't want her any more. Her own family were a very bad one.

She confided in Jessica about something – that she didn't believe in God. She was a complete atheist.

One day Jessica heard shouting from the Mother Superior. It wasn't like her to get angry like that, and at the same time she was highly sympathetic towards Maria. She had been out that day looking for a job with children and had got just the post she wanted, with the right hours and conditions. The woman said, "You are going to come aren't you? Only so often they say they will and then I'm lucky if they phone me up and tell me they're not taking the job."

"I promise you I'll come" said Maria.

The husband offered her a lift to the station. When they were alone in the car he said he'd double her wages for her and made a pass at her at the same time. She knew she couldn't go. She now knew why so many other girls had let his wife down by pulling out of taking the job. The Mother Superior told her, "You are to phone up that woman and tell her the true reason why you're not going".

She was very sympathetic towards the wife as well, and Maria very reluctantly did as she told her. The wife just quietly accepted it. Shortly after this Maria started to do her training to be a nursery nurse at Ingledene, a children's home on Richmond Road, Bowdon.

Meanwhile a new nun had arrived, Sister Jean. She was in a bad mood because she'd failed her driving test. She said it was because she had thought she was in a row of stationary cars and she wasn't, and she had parked there. Yet Sister Jean should have been happy that she could at least drive. She had once thought that the day would never come; she just could not get the hang of it.

Then she heard about someone else who had passed, even though he had been a dreadful driver. It made her furious. She knew how he'd passed – he didn't mind a bit of scrounging and he'd been out practising with someone who was generous. Sister Jean was there to take orders, not to give them, yet she complained so bitterly to the church about this that it was arranged for her to have enough driving lessons to enable her to pass her test, which she did second time.

Jessica heard about some other care homes which were very bad places. It broke her heart to hear that residents could practically be thrown out of bed in the mornings and be roughly handled before being thrown into the bath. They would be shouted at and insulted. One carer told her it was noticeable that the ones who hadn't had their breakfast that morning would quarrel among themselves, sometimes even having a stand-up row in the middle of the ward.

"How do you know they've had no breakfast?" asked Jessica.

"They live in the nurses' home and they don't turn up in the canteen for it because they've got up too late. Then they take it off the trolley when the breakfast comes up for the patients, it would be thrown away otherwise. They take it into some quiet cubicle to be on their own, but they have to make sure they're not caught. It's a deadly sin to be found eating food on the ward if it was intended for the patients."

She was also told the part-time carers had most patience with the patients, which might be why people like Jessica were encouraged to come in. Even if it was only for one day a week, their help made it much easier to manage, especially with lifting and bathing. It meant it was only a small part of your life, not your whole way of life. Maybe the Mother Superior knew all this, and that was why she had so many part-time staff and allowed them to buy their meals there. They didn't have to pay much, and Jessica would get the money back off her grandmother.

One day one of the carers asked Jessica to help lift a patient. The woman was already sitting on the edge of the bed, so Jessica agreed and tried to help. They struggled and struggled but just couldn't manage it, even though the woman was being perfectly co-operative and wasn't particularly heavy. Both of the carers were by now quite experienced.

The patient said, "Oh well never mind, I will just have to stay in bed for longer today." Jessica said to the other carer, "You were trying to get her out, were you? I was trying to get her in!"

They had another resident arrive, a Mrs Thomas, and for the second time Jessica saw an appalling bedsore. This time it was on her back and was deeply ulcerated. Jessica was learning fast, for when she first started working there she didn't even know there was such a thing. They had to explain to her that bedsores happen if you leave a person lying or sitting in the same position for too long. She now knew that if there was any sign of broken skin you had to report it at once to a nurse. Once they start they take a long time to heal. The Mother Superior seemed to think it might never heal completely.

They talked about how they would have to make certain Mrs Thomas was kept out of bed as much as possible and regularly turned when in bed. If she was sitting in a chair, she was not to be in the same position the whole of the time. There was no trouble getting her to walk with a zimmer frame, although she was very slow.

Mrs Thomas was very curious. For example, she stopped to have a good look in the kitchen at a man who was defrosting the fridge. She looked out of the window to see the people going down to the River Bollin, and she saw a teddy boy going past with a blonde. It was all keeping her on her feet and off her back.

Jessica didn't like teddy boys at all and nor did Peggy, yet they were only going by hearsay. Some of them were all right, according to a retired schoolteacher who had taught infants. They would hang around in large numbers – she wouldn't call it gangs – and sometimes when she was in Woolworths, they would nod a friendly hello to her.

She didn't recognize them, but they clearly knew her. She felt certain she had taught some of them and that as she hadn't changed in the last ten years, they still knew her, but she would no longer recognize them. She wrote to the papers about it to contradict what other people were saying. "Teddy boys are friendly young men" she wrote.

The River Bollin would attract a lot of people, including young lovers and lads from the inner city who would come at weekends and camp there. Some of them were very rough and would give the rest a bad name. One woman lost the sign for her house, 'Waldon', and never suspected it was they who had taken it until it was seen nailed up on a tree by the Bollin.

Another man went down there to tell one of them to keep away from his daughter, who was sixteen. The youth shouted back at him, "What makes you think you're so good yourself?" After this the man forbade her to see him. He wouldn't let her go down to the river at all, and she didn't speak to either of her parents for two days after.

Jessica and Peggy loved hearing about things like this, but they weren't going to go themselves. Then everything cheered up when the book *Lady Chatterley's Lover* came out. There had been so much publicity about it; they thought it was going to be censored, but the publishers won a court case and it was published, so everyone went rushing out to buy it. Of course Maria had to keep that well hidden in the convent.

Peggy meanwhile got another job giving out newspapers. She delivered every morning before breakfast around the big houses in Hale, cycling up their big drives. Mrs Newton loved hearing all about it after Peggy had arrived back before breakfast and could tell her about things that were going on out in the world while she was still in bed.

Peggy would start at seven in the morning and get eleven shillings and sixpence a week. It was good money, as most shops only paid seven and six, but then those shops didn't expect the paper boy or girl to sort them out before they delivered them; they would arrive at the shop and it was done. She found it fun being with them all as they worked away and seeing what was going on in the shop. She didn't know then, but that was how work should be, something to be enjoyed. As a result, they did a good job and no one was complaining that they didn't get their newspaper.

There had been quite a bit in the papers about a man who had gone missing, from a big house where Peggy delivered. He was 35 and had been depressed for some time about business problems. Then the newspapers all reported that his body had been found – he had drowned himself. She had to cycle up the drive to the big house where he had lived and put this news through his letterbox for all his family to read. Of course, she realised they would all already know, but she still hated it.

People seem to find anything that takes away dignity amusing, and love to overthrow authority. When Peggy was sorting out the newspapers she noticed a report of a local case where a judge had spent all day in court telling everyone else what to do. As she went to school with two of his daughter she knew for a fact that when he got home that night there was a letter waiting for him telling him to get his kids to school on time.

The newsagent's wife was a scatterbrain and never put things back where she found them. She was always looking for such things as pens. When Peggy told her grandmother this and said "Her trouble is she doesn't put things back", it amused her, for she was always telling Peggy to do this. In her job she was finding out how wise this advice was. Work had to be done by a certain time.

The newsagent's wife was always in a dither. Early in the morning the newsagent would be calling up the stairs to her to hurry up, and it would greatly amuse all the kids who were sorting out the newspapers. Anyone who didn't know her would imagine she was being very selfish – here was her husband needing her so much and there was she taking her time in coming – but it was no such thing. Whatever she was doing, she was in a dreadful flap about it.

One time he was very angry with his son, who also worked there, because a customer had come in and left again because he couldn't get served. The man had thought he was being very considerate in going, and that he had chosen an awkward moment. He did not know there was always some sort of a flap going on. Once during a flap, the mother had said to the son "there's no need to shout!" When Peggy told her grandmother about it she seized the opportunity to agree for she was always telling Peggy this.

Another time Peggy's bicycle was stolen. The police got it back for her and she had to go down to the police station to get it. "You've come very early" they said, and she told them she was about to start a round. When they asked her what time that would be, she knew to say seven o'clock. It was against the law to let them begin sorting before then, though he would let them sometimes.

Chapter Seven

RETURN TO LONDON 1665

Catherine still visited them very frequently, sometimes staying the night, but she also spent a lot of time at Willow Tree Cottage. She yearned to go back into London in her own time, so one day the three of them decided to return.

They went down the steps again, through the door, and there they were again in the London of 1665. They walked through the usual streets, but how their hearts sank. Houses were closed up, there were crosses on doors and notices up on some of them saying "Lord have mercy upon us". The plague had arrived.

They saw one poor soul lying down in an alleyway, very near to death. They passed a man dressed up in the most peculiar clothes who looked as though he was on his way somewhere. Catherine explained that he was a doctor and had to dress like that in order to protect himself. She said, "The plague is caused by bad smells in the air, so he has to wear clothes to protect him while he's seeing to the patients. He has to have a special mask with goggles to protect his eyes, a beak filled with herbs to cover bad smells, thick gloves to protect his hands and a coat covered in wax to keep out bad air."

When they reached Catherine's mother's house, she was standing there waiting for her daughter. "Oh Catherine I have been so worried about you, I thought you had died in the plague!" she said. They went inside and she told her daughter she was sending her away.

"Oh please don't do that to me mother, I always do what you say!"

"You can't stay in London."

Jessica and Peggy realised this was a lot more serious than when polio had struck Altrincham and they had not been allowed to go to the pictures, where it would spread.

"But mother, I have always done what you have told me to do to avoid it" Catherine protested, and indeed she had. In fact while they were there, her mother put some herbs into a pot and poured boiling water on to them. She then spooned out some black sticky stuff from a jar and held it out to her. It was walnuts and treacle. Catherine was used to regular doses of it; she knew it was supposed to protect her from the plague.

But now things were very serious indeed and her mother felt that Catherine had to leave London. Hundreds of people had died. People with money were loading their belongings on to carts and moving out into the country. Others stayed to look after their businesses and shops. Poor people had no choice but to stay. It was bad news for beggars that so many people with money were leaving, as they depended upon their gifts.

"Where are you going to send me?" Catherine asked.

"To Bowdon. You've got to stay with your Aunt Heather where it's safe."

"I've said I don't want to go!"

"I'm telling you you've got to."

"It may not be safe to go there. There may be highwaymen on the way."

"You'll be all right. We'll send you with more than one person who has a gun on them."

"I still don't want to go." There was another reason; she didn't want to leave Ginger.

Peggy asked her, "Will you make her go if I tell you that I know for a fact that she will die of the plague if she goes to Bowdon?"

"But you can't tell me that."

Peggy carefully spelt it out to her. "If Catherine goes to Bowdon she'll die of the plague. She'll be buried in Bowdon Churchyard."

Catherine's mother put her arm round Catherine as though to protect her from these two "mad and dangerous" girls. She said to them, "You had better go now." She looked as if she might get angry, so they went.

The walk back through the streets was horrendous. They saw many terrible things. One woman called to them from an upstairs window to ask if they had any food on them. They hadn't. "How have you been getting it before?" They asked her. She told them she could lower a basket from the upstairs window on a rope, it had money in it and she could tell the watchman what she wanted. She also said there were pigeons in the loft, a smelly and messy place but they seemed happy enough and she would sometimes take one to eat. Jessica and Peggy went on their way and when they looked round she was lowering her basket, for the watchman had arrived.

Food had become difficult to come by as traders were afraid to go to the city and there were many fewer boats on the River Thames.

The streets were almost deserted, and those who did venture out kept themselves to themselves. The women hid their faces behind poseys and herbs, while the men had their clothes wrapped round their faces up to their eyes.

The girls walked on and then they came face to face with Elizabeth, Catherine's friend. She looked as though she felt free and then she told them why. "I have my precious certificate" she said. She had been up to the Old Bailey to get it. She had needed it because an old aunt of hers had died of the plague in the house where she was living, so she had been not allowed to leave the house for 40 days after. Then, if she still hadn't got it she could get a doctor's certificate to say she was safe. She read it out to them:

> *"This is to confirm that Elizabeth Wickham has not succumbed the plague and is of sound health. She has resided for 40 days and nights in the house in which her aunt died of it."*
>
> *Andrew Portal, Physician, 13th April 1665*

She told them how wicked some people were. "There were more than 100 people outside the Old Bailey waiting in a queue. The clerk was reading all the letters carefully and told the man in front of me that there was no doctor with the name on the certificate. The man began to argue. The clerk asked him how much he had paid for it, as it seemed he had been cheated; someone had pretended to be a doctor. Either that or this man had broken out of a locked house and written it himself."

It was now beginning to get dark, and everyone had to be in by nine. They walked on. As they went along the cobbled street, they could hear a cart rattle on the cobblestones and a voice calling out, "Bring out your dead!"

The church bell was tolling the whole of the time. There was a belief that this would frighten the plague away, and for the same reason every now and again a cannon would be fired. They heard of some other funny ideas – some people had put notices up about them. For one thing they seemed to think that anything that was touched by water was a danger. The instructions would include such things as not eating chicken, duck, goose, fish, pig, old beef or fat meat. Then they would go on to say, don't sleep during the day, don't take much exercise, don't cook in rainwater, don't have a bath, don't think about death, only think about pleasant things, visit beautiful gardens and look at the scenery or look at silver and gold.

They were stopping to help people pick up the bodies of people who had died out on the street. What good did that do, they wondered? It was said that the dead were killing the living. Everyone was very upset. Jessica put her arm round one distraught woman whose daughter had just died. No one tried to stop her, yet the woman shouldn't really have been out on the street. Her house was one of many that was shut up. Jessica knew she was immune to the disease and that it could not harm her. Then, when they helped the man put another body on to the cart, someone called across to them, "Don't do that, you'll get it yourself".

The man driving the cart would ring a bell and call out, "Bring out the dead!" Jessica and Peggy worked all night, going into people's houses, dark now that the shutters were kept permanently closed and the only lighting they had was either a candle or a lantern.

"God bless you" the people would say to her in their pitiful voices and put their hands out to her to get some comfort. When she touched them they would say, "You're very kind".

"I'll pray for you" she heard one distraught voice call out to them; it was someone passing in the street. They had seen that the house was shut up, the shutters closed and a cross on the door. The man on the cart said, "Get inside, it's gone nine."

Eventually it started to get light and it was time for them to go. The cart had to be off the road. Then they heard a man's voice call across to them loud and clear, "Go away, go away or you'll catch it!" It was the doctor they had seen before all dressed up in funny clothes. He bawled at them "Keep yourself safe!"

He had been so busy himself that night. He was trying everything, sweating and blistering the patients as well as leeching them. There was a belief that burning incense would do some good, but he had long given up on that, as he found that it didn't work for him.

Jessica and Peggy didn't do what the doctor told them to do straight away. A woman was staggering about to get back inside her home. She was about to collapse on to the ground, and she looked at them both with pleading eyes. Jessica and Peggy both gently nodded to her. "Yes we will help you", said Peggy.

They held her up and led her slowly into the house. It was almost dark but it was how she wanted it, as she could no longer stand the light. They laid her down on a mattress on the floor and gave her a cup of water. She desperately wanted it, but was too weak to take it herself; she couldn't even hold the cup to her mouth. Jessica held her hand as she saw her take her last breath. They hoped she died at least in some comfort in the peace of her own home.

Sadly they walked out of the house, only to hear crying from next door. There was a cross on the door. They went inside to find an old man just leaving. His wife had told him to go as she lay there dying on a filthy straw mattress. Clearly she was in pain.

The old man looked around him at the wooden walls and stone floor; he opened the door slowly and said, "They'll stop me if they catch me." His wife said nothing.

The street was now empty. The old man clutched the bundle of food and the few coins he had on him and wondered how he could do such a thing as leave his wife, but he knew it was no good, she would die and he would too if he didn't go. He limped out on to the street, turning his head away from the pile of bodies at the corner. People were dying faster than they could carry them and huge pits were filled with corpses and covered over, but there were fresh corpses in the street. They had been left there for the cart to come and carry them away. The idea was that people stayed inside their houses until nine at night and then brought out the bodies, but it couldn't be organized that way, it was far too much to manage.

As the old man shuffled down the street a bell clanged and a voice shouted, "Bring out your dead!" He managed to get out of the stinking city. He sat beside a hedge and felt a lot better breathing in the grassy air. After a few bites of the dry bread from his pack he lay down and thought about his wife. How could he have gone? Who were those girls who were staying with her? They said they were immune to the plague.

He fell asleep and began to have a nightmare. He saw bodies bloated and blue, he saw the devil, he saw hell, he saw a bottomless pit. Then he screamed and woke. He lay there for a while, realising he was in the country when a wagon of hay came past.

"Going far?" the driver asked him.

"I don't know where I'm going" he replied.

They travelled for two days before they reached an ancient town. He remembered it well – it was where he'd been brought up, where he'd been happy, but now people were spitting fear.

"We don't want you here!" they were saying. A crowd had gathered.

"I'm not from London" he told them.

They didn't believe him. He tried giving them money, but was told they didn't want it. One woman bent down to pick up a stone to throw at him. "This is a clean town here!" she shouted. As he left they chucked pebbles at him.

He found an old shepherd's hut with a leaking roof, where he lay on the earth floor and tried to get some sleep. Then the sweating started; the pains in his armpits and his head burnt with fever. He wanted water, but even if he had had some he would have been too weak to drink it. He wished he hadn't left his wife, they could have died together. He knew he had the plague.

Meanwhile his wife had died. "You're very kind" were the woman's last words to her. Then the voice came again, "Bring out your dead!" and Peggy and Jessica carried the woman out.

They walked briskly back to the door, on their way back to the Devisdale. On the way they saw a child being brought crying out of a house with only a blanket wrapped round her. She was shortly to be given a new set of clothes, plague free, as she hadn't got the plague herself. Where were they taking her?

The woman by her side signalled to them both to be quiet. She was going to the country, but both her parents had the plague, the house was shut up and no one was supposed to leave it. Written on the door were as usual the words "Lord have mercy upon us." Her parents were both inside. Jessica and Peggy looked at the child. She was shortly to be orphaned, yet she still had hope. They continued on their way back to the Devisdale.

Both girls would shortly be leaving school. Just before they went another girl was expelled, Marion Carter. She had been very trying for some time, and then one day she said in the classroom in front of everyone, "My father's coming up this weekend with his final complaints about the school." The teacher in the room overheard and said, "Well your father won't have a leg to stand on". She said he would be totally in the wrong.

When she began to argue, the teacher asked what his complaints were going to be and Marion said that besides everything else there weren't enough playing fields. That was only one absurd comment she made, for firstly there were plenty, and secondly she was no great sportswoman anyway.

After the teacher had left the room, the head teacher came bursting in. She was fuming. She wanted to make it very clear to everyone that whenever Mr Carter came up to the school it was for nothing else but to apologise and that he was always most humble. She had phoned him up. She had managed to get him straight away, and he had agreed with everything she said. But then he would, with the mood she was in.

The head teacher ranted on. "We both agree that he's got the most impossible daughter. There isn't a more impossible girl from here to the other side of Birmingham."

She went on to say that Marion was going; she wasn't going to have her any more. She'd been expelled. However, she didn't leave in the end. Mr Carter managed to talk the head round. Some people said she had made herself look silly, that she should have stuck to her word, but others disagreed. She had certainly got what she wanted. She had got everyone to see that whenever Mr Carter came up to the school it was she who did the complaining and he who did the apologising.

Jessica knew what to do, as the Mother Superior kept phoning her up and asking her to go in. She got to know the place quite well. There was quite a bit of coming and going, and the residents were complaining that staff kept changing; maybe this was why Jessica was called upon so often, because they knew her. There were new nuns working there, young ones, typically young, giggly and lively, and Jessica felt so at home with them that sometimes she would start talking to them about nuns, forgetting they were nuns themselves.

One evening she was walking along a short corridor when one of the old ladies, Mrs Smith, took a vase she had been carrying out of her hand. She was swinging it from side to side and singing at the same time as though she was at a party. Jessica would have thought no more about it, but for something that happened that evening at bedtime. Sister St Clare was taking Mrs Smith to her bed, linking arms, and the old lady was still singing away. Sister St Clare said to Jessica, "I don't know what this doctor has given this woman but clearly she can't take it, she's drunk."

Next day she heard the Mother Superior talking on the phone to one of the doctors about it. "Please take care what you give her" she said. "Clearly she's very sensitive to it and we've had her drunk and disorderly."

Those words came back a couple of years later when Jessica was training to be a nurse. A tutor stood up in the classroom in front of them all and said, "It's not just newspaper talk, they say we're about to face a big drug problem and that it will no longer be something that's unheard of. It's unthinkable. Things can go so very wrong, even when drugs are properly prescribed by a doctor. Whatever is going to happen, if we have idiots dishing them out whose only interest is the money?"

But for now Jessica was working in the home. She had people on her back nagging her to think about her future, and saying she should do some training. She went to Altrincham Hospital as a cadet. She found the work a lot easier, as there was not nearly so much heavy lifting and the patients were usually less confused and more co-operative. A lot of the work was just making beds, arranging flowers, giving out drinks and taking temperatures.

Sister Edwards was the ward dragon, and Jessica found her one big joke. She was told she had to show respect. She was to let her walk out of the door first and sometimes even open it for her. Jessica did open it for her once, then "accidentally" closed it when she was half way through. After doing other things like this she realised that she had managed to intimidate the woman a little. Maybe she was afraid she'd have a revolt on her hands.

Jessica had once put her foot out as though to trip her up and then said, "Oh sorry Sister, I was just having a look to see if my shoes need polishing."

Peggy meanwhile got a job in a small clothes shop in Deansgate in Manchester. They had to tell the customers how nice they looked in what they tried on regardless of how ghastly it was, until one day a woman said to Peggy, "Oh you do tell such lies!"

"The customer is always right" replied Peggy. The manageress had told her to do it.

It was shortly after this that they opened a new Marks and Spencer nearby, so she was out of work. Other things started going wrong, but she didn't realise until afterwards that it was because the management wanted to get rid of the staff, because the money was no longer coming in. The heating wasn't working and they all nearly froze. It was a very cold winter. The staff who worked upstairs thought the manageress wasn't taking it seriously, only to find that she was, that this was one thing she wasn't guilty of. They knew because when she was talking on the phone they would pin their ears to the wall and hear what she was saying. Even Peggy didn't know they were doing this until she went upstairs one day and saw them.

One problem with being cold is that it makes people quarrelsome. The management, apart from the manageress, weren't trying to get the heating mended. They did put a heater into the changing room so that the customers would be warm when trying something on, but one of the girls took it out and put it into the shop. She expected to be told she couldn't do this and she was ready for a stand-up row about it, yet surprisingly not a thing was said to her, so in the shop the heater stayed.

Peggy wasn't allowed to sit down. She knew this was wrong, and that there were laws that could protect her, as it was well known that shop girls get varicose veins. The laws had been made in the early 1900s or before, but they were not being observed here. She didn't say anything.

They continued to try to sell things. The manageress wasn't allowed to say what stock they should order, although she knew what the customers were asking for. Peggy knew that their wages came out of what they sold and if they didn't sell enough there wouldn't be the money to pay them.

Peggy was told they used to keep a row of labels under the counter and slip one on to a garment to match the size the customer had asked for. They justified it by saying they could bring it back if it didn't fit and change it for something else. That was what the customers did. Then they started getting stock in with labels sewn on. They found a way round it, until someone complained and there was a big row. They all still denied they'd ever done it, and they were good at pretending to be indignant.

Jessica was transferred to Denzell, along Green Walk, where a mansion had been converted into a hospital for rehabilitation. The work here was easier still. Starting on the same day was a young auxiliary nurse called Lucy, who had never worked in a hospital or anywhere like it before.

One thing Jessica immediately learnt was not to get common sense mixed up with common knowledge. When Sister asked Lucy to take the flowers out she didn't say out of the ward and into the sluice, and as Lucy had already seen them there she assumed she meant out of the sluice and into the ward. She did as she was told. A little later Sister asked her to do this again and when Lucy told her she had already done it she looked surprised, but accepted it. Then shortly after Lucy went into the sluice to find them there again, so she started taking them back into the ward. It took them a bit of time to realise that while Jessica was taking them one way Lucy was taking them the other. Her defence would have been, "Sister, you said take the flowers out, you didn't say out of the ward and into the sluice".

One night when Jessica was walking home, she noticed a young female doctor walking along Green Walk. As she started crossing the road she fell flat on her face – she was drunk. Her immediate thought was to shout out something provocative, yet something seemed to tell her it was serious. In any case, she wouldn't dare, not to someone so senior, despite what she had done to the other sister on the ward.

Clearly the doctor thought no one had seen her fall. Jessica hid in the background and watched her staggering up against a wall, being sick. She then fell down again. It's difficult to go up and help someone like that, and yet it can be difficult not to. As soon as the doctor was back on her feet and staggering away, Jessica ran for it. She felt certain the doctor hadn't seen her and wouldn't have wanted Jessica to have seen what happened. Little did Jessica know that this woman would never work as a doctor again. She took the next day off, went to see her own doctor, and told him she was an alcoholic.

The girls were missing Catherine very much, and wondered if there was any point in going back to London in 1665 without her. They felt certain that if they did go, they would never find her, yet they decided to give it a try anyway.

They left very early in the morning before work, feeling confident about going without her, as they had done it so many times before. They went through the door at the bottom wondering what they might see. There might be nothing at all. It might be just a hole in the ground, now that they no longer had Catherine with them.

But they were not disappointed, and soon found themselves back in London just as before. It was very early in the morning there, too; most of the people hadn't got out of bed. The girls strolled through the streets they now knew so well. They passed the baker's, which was now lit up with a lantern, and saw a notice which said "Breadmaker for the King."

They were now much more wary as they stepped between the puddles and piles of rubbish littering the narrow streets. Now and then they glanced up at balconies overhead. Even that early in the morning people would throw dirty water out of them, and worse.

They also now knew not to get close to dark alleyways, as robbers would wait there. It was strange that they were getting so streetwise in London 1666, but much less so to the Altrincham of 1959; in fact Catherine was more aware than they were in Altrincham, having slept rough there.

They strolled down to the River Thames. Although it was early in the morning, it seemed to be very busy, like the streets of some big city like Manchester, everyone getting ready for the day ahead of them. They sat and watched it all, boats and barges being loaded and going up and down. Then suddenly they heard a voice call out "Fire! Fire! Fetch the Mayor!"

"It's the Great Fire of London starting" cried out Jessica. "Quick, back to 1959, or we'll be stuck here if our staircase is burned down. Look at how its spreading!"

The sky was black with smoke, and they started to run. It must have seemed strange to other people that they were running in the opposite direction from everyone else. The street was full of horses running, the heat driving them all towards the river. As they ran people were jumping out of windows. They paused to help someone who was struggling hard to get out of a little window, with flames licking up not far behind them.

Jessica and Peggy continued to run and run. Fire was spreading very quickly from one roof to another until every roof was ablaze. Young mothers were running for their lives, hugging their howling babies, young children running along by their side. Everyone had their night clothes on. They were also very keen to get their belongings somewhere safe, but Jessica and Peggy had to think about themselves and getting back to the Devisdale, for although their staircase was of stone and couldn't burn, something else might happen to prevent them going. They noticed as they tore through the streets how many people were clinging to their valuables as they hurried to safety.

They came to the street where they could get back up to the Devisdale, which was ablaze and completely deserted. Luckily, the door they needed was untouched. They ran straight through it and up the steps to the Devisdale, then tore out of the house and the tree shouting "Fire, Fire!" People out taking their dogs for a walk turned to stare at them. Clearly they had seen something very frightening.

When they got home the girls told their grandmother that they had seen a dreadful road accident, that a car had caught fire and they had only just got the driver out in time. They had to say something, or she would ask them why they weren't going into work. They were too upset to go.

Chapter Eight

THE TRIALS OF NURSING

Surprisingly, Jessica passed the entrance examination for training as an SRN. She went to Chester Royal Infirmary, where she spent much of the first three months in the classroom. It was quite chilly and difficult to wrap up warm, as they had to wear uniform. The Sister Tutor was sympathetic and said that they should be allowed to wear a woolly jumper and that she would speak to the Matron about it. The response she got was a cold one: "Not until they wear a vest" she was told. Until not so long ago everyone had worn vests and it was news to the Sister Tutor that they were now considered old fashioned. Puzzled, she asked the girls if this was true and then meekly told them not to let her do that again, for they had made her feel very silly, asking if they could wear jumpers.

The first thing they learned about was bedsores. The tutor was giving a list of causes of them and they were writing them down. She made them all write at the top of the page, with nothing to dilute it, "bad nursing". This of course is right, no hiding the truth, but later she was to discover that discipline in other areas was completely crazy, yet at the same time not to comply would be slapping them across the face. It was so very much the considered thing. If they saw a sister coming they were expected to open the door for her to walk through, so Jessica always made certain she didn't see them coming. Then late one evening after having worked on the ward all day she was in the nurses' home, and a lot of them were in their dressing gowns and ready for bed, but not Jessica. She was still in her full uniform, cap, apron and cloak leaning against the wall next to the door laughing and joking with some other nurses when the night sister came down the corridor. Jessica meekly opened the door for her, as it would have been cocking a snook at her not to, and the sister merely said "Thank you" as she walked through.

Next morning on the ward she met the sister again, to find that she certainly didn't think that no sister could do any wrong. She was giving the report to the day sister with the rest of the student nurses present, but it was with great difficulty as the day sister kept coughing, almost choking at times.

"Have you finished?" the night sister asked her, sounding like a ferocious school teacher in a class room. She turned round to the junior nurses and gently told them "This is smoking, you know!"

The day sister hadn't finished. She continued to cough away while the night sister continued to glare at her, and then after a minute or two she finally stopped. The night sister, still glaring at her and still sounding like an angry teacher, asked her, "Can I get on with the report now?"

Jessica could not manage the rest of the paperwork, and failed the exam at the end of it. They let her work on the ward for three months after that and take the exam again, but she failed once more, so they booted her out. She went to do her State Enrolled Nurse course instead in Stockport. This was a two-year practical course with more emphasis on bedside nursing. SENs were very much looked down upon. There was serious discrimination and a lot of them were made to feel very small. Once something starts it is very difficult to stop; people follow one another like sheep.

The nurses in charge, such as the matron and the assistant matron, as it was in those days, tried so hard to give them confidence, to tell them that they were good, that they were very busy making people comfortable in their beds, but it was the idiots who seemed to have the most influence and many of the nurses training to do their SEN found they couldn't ignore it.

Those training to be SENs spent a lot of time on the geriatric unit at St. Thomas's on Shaw Heath next to Our Lady's Church, but it wasn't all dull. One old man had some terminal illness and would never be coming out of hospital. He had been living with a much younger woman for many years and bringing up a family. In those days it wasn't just taboo but also quite serious, as it meant his partner wouldn't be entitled to a widow's pension, and also it would greatly affect any benefits for the children. He was told they would have to get married. The hospital chaplain said he could do it, but there was some complication as to how much it would cost and they hadn't got the money. Consequently an ambulance had to be brought and he was taken to the church. Don't ask me how they managed that one, to get an ambulance for a wedding, but they did. When he arrived back one nurse called out to another nurse, Mary, "Bridegroom's back!" It was a sarcastic comment that Mary only half laughed at; she clearly knew it was no joke.

People were a lot more optimistic about another wedding that took place in Our Lady's Church just next door. An SEN was marrying a young police officer and afterwards, all dressed up in her wedding dress, she came on to the ward, now a female one, with the bridegroom to visit the patients. They all just loved it.

After a short time at St. Thomas's, Jessica was moved to Stepping Hill to work on a ward which was largely orthopaedic. Many of the patients were old women with broken hips needing pinning and plating, and the work was exhausting; it involved a lot of lifting and a lot of patience.

Quite a few of the patients on this ward were very confused, and most of them were very old indeed. One morning when they were taking the report, the night nurse said a woman with a fractured femur had been brought in. They all screamed. They felt they couldn't take any more. Then the nurse hurriedly added, "No it's all right, she's young, she's only seventy-four." They all burst out laughing. After this the patient was nick named "Youngie".

It wasn't unusual for the night sister to be told when doing her round, "This girl had a terrible night, she's not been to bed once." They clearly didn't know where they were or who the nurses were. In fact it wasn't unusual for them to think they were family, calling them by a family name and sometimes even ticking them off about something.

Then Jessica was put on nights, and her shifts were far from quiet. One of the old ladies kept the whole ward wide awake and was very confused, shouting, "Everybody up, everyone get out of bed!" She refused to be quiet, so the night sister was brought, but she couldn't do anything with her either and all the old lady would say to her was "No I won't, no I shan't". It amused Jessica to see such cheek being given to Sister, but she could also see that Sister couldn't keep her face straight either. She started to giggle like a silly girl. The noise was so bad that eventually lights went on everywhere. A patient went into the kitchen, made a big pot of tea and pushed the trolley down the ward to give everyone a cup.

CHAPTER EIGHT

At least the old ladies didn't spend all their time talking about going home; on the contrary, they wanted to stay. The relatives too liked it, seeing that they were beginning to settle so well, and they had to be told they couldn't do that because the beds would be needed for someone else. Stepping Hill was the last place the nurses would want to make into their home. It frustrated the ward sister, because she had previously owned a nursing home, and had tried hard to make it into a home but failed. None of them wanted to stay. They spent the whole of the time talking about going home. Jessica wondered if there was some connection, if it was the fact that they couldn't go that was making them want to so much.

She also worked on a men's ward, largely to do with orthopaedics. One day a young man who had been working on a building site was brought in with a cracked vertebra. He was put on a special mattress, the idea being to stop it breaking completely and making him a paraplegic for life, but it seemed to be having the opposite effect. While his wife sat by his bedside gently telling him to keep still and Jessica and another nurse stood there saying the same he was nevertheless doing his best to toss about. This could make the break more serious, but his point was that he couldn't help it, as it was so uncomfortable to be in a bed like that.

"We'll have to take him out of it and put him in an ordinary one" Jessica said to the other nurse. A young doctor standing not far away overheard her.

"No, he can't be!" he called across to them.

"But he won't stay still if we keep him in this one" Jessica told him.

"He bloody well will do!" barked the doctor, for things had been hectic on that ward all morning and everyone was on edge. Unfortunately, the patient overheard him. How could a man lying there so helpless manage to give him such a mouthful? And yet he did.

141

"We'll bloody well swap roles!" he shouted across to him. "You bloody well lie still in this bed all day and I'll be the bloody doctor!"

Although his wife remained there looking most docile, they had swapped roles all right, but not in the way he had suggested. It was now the patient who was giving out the orders while the doctor and Jessica stood to attention.

After this Jessica worked in Casualty. Early one morning a paper boy was brought in; he had walked in on a burglary and the robbers had made a dreadful mess of him. He was unconscious with head injuries. It was even suspected that he knew the robbers and they wanted to silence him, but had been disturbed by someone else and had to run for it. It was a planned burglary in a wealthy property. It was obvious that it had been done by professional criminals. Jessica thought about Peggy and how she'd been delivering papers in a very good area. It was really coming to something if you couldn't allow a kid do the job in case something like this happened. Fortunately, when he came round it emerged that he did know one of them, and consequently all of them were caught.

Then another youth was brought in who had fallen down a fire exit. He was clearly in severe pain and crying out for something to relieve it, but with head injuries, it can be difficult to tell whether the drugs are making them confused or it's the head injuries, so they can't have any medication. It seemed heartless to Jessica.

Suddenly, the doctor exclaimed in the most unprofessional manner, "Oh don't tell me we've got a junkie here just out to get his next fix."

Jessica was horrified. Did they do that – deliberately injure themselves for a fix? She was told they did. She felt as though this new problem of drugs was invading her life, for that evening she had a phone call from a friend to say her house had been broken into by junkies. It was going on everywhere. An addict would be desperate to get anything to pay for his habit. Now people had to do so much more to secure their houses. One person said, "Are we going to go back to the Middle Ages?" She didn't know that Jessica had been back to the 17th century and had been involved in a stagecoach robbery.

If she hadn't been put off driving a car by her motorbike accident, she would certainly have been put off by this. She felt at times as though she didn't even want to be a passenger in a car. She wondered why they didn't make it compulsory to wear a seat belt in a car and a crash helmet on a motorbike. It seemed sheer madness not to. She was once with some people who were talking in Italian about Italy, but she couldn't understand what they were saying. They told her that in Italy you were allowed to ride a motorbike at 14. Then she found she could understand one word of Italian, which was "ridiculo". She knew how bad she and Peggy had been on their bicycles at this age in Hale. Whatever would they have been like amongst all the traffic on a motorbike in Rome? Had the people who made this law never been 14 themselves?

Some years later she heard a youth talking with contempt about "middle-aged men in suits who sit round tables making up laws". He then went on to say that when you looked into it, you would find that they themselves had not ridden a motorbike for twenty-odd years. He didn't seem to realise that there might be some connection, and that this might be why they were making up all these regulations. They knew so much. She'd come off a motor bike and put herself in hospital when very young. A brain surgeon from Manchester Royal Infirmary was quoted in the papers as saying that motorbikes should be banned from the roads altogether.

She lived in the nurses' home and would sometimes not go out of the hospital grounds for days, but she did once spend all night at the house of a friend, who gave her a lift into work next morning. She was on the roads among all the other people going to work. She realised that this was how most people lived, but it was so different to her own life. She saw cars whizzing round roundabouts, people stopping to pick one another up. It was ordinary, good drivers she was seeing, yet it didn't stop her thinking, "Please don't have an accident". She didn't want to meet them shortly in casualty.

She knew someone who was talking about moving. They didn't know whether to stay where they were or move nearer to where he worked. Jessica asked her if it had occurred to her that if his car went wrong in Hale Barns, he would be stuck. She was told he wouldn't because the firm would immediately lay on another one. She never considered for a second that if he was going to be driving on the motorway every day for an hour for maybe the next 30 years, sooner or later something might happen.

She saw what a mess an illegal abortion could cause. She wished there was more money around to prevent women doing it. She was horrified when she heard they were talking about solving the problem by making it legal to kill a foetus. She wondered how much all that would cost the NHS. She thought of all the ways the money could be spent if it went on preventing unwanted pregnancies instead.

She saw battered women come in. She had thought before it was only obvious roughheads who were knocking their wives about, no one of any class would do such a thing, but she learned that it was not so. It was going on across all classes. It wasn't simple and straightforward.

She would sometimes see battered men. One had a cut in the eye done by a woman with a piece of broken glass – he could have lost the sight in it. Although of course that was taken very seriously,

Jessica wondered why it was considered funny if a woman was battering her husband, just as long as no harm came of it.

That night she went to the pictures with a nurse who also worked in Casualty and they laughed and laughed. The film was all about comic strip women with sleeves rolled up, wielding rolling pins. The film wasn't realistic – what the women were doing was barely physically possible. For a start there was no such thing as a typical man, men were not all the same, and yet here, in this factory, although they certainly didn't have mobile phones in those days, they all agreed at the same time to phone their wives and say they were working late when really they were going to see a show with pretty girls dancing on the stage. You would never get all the men in one place of work to agree upon that, they're not all the same, but it makes a good joke if it's a film about the battle of the sexes.

The film didn't explain how they'd managed to all get washed and changed into suits so quickly, nor was it realistic the way they managed to hire a coach within such a short time. Yet they did so, leaving their wives at home to watch television.

The television cameras were there at the show. They showed the girls dancing on the stage and then there was a shot of the audience, a row of all these men enjoying themselves. Then the film showed the wives at home watching television and seeing their husbands there. What followed was hard to believe. All the women managed to be in the bus station when the coach rolled in at the end of the night. There they were all waiting for them with sleeves rolled up and with rolling pins, saucepans and frying pans, just anything to attack them with. Jessica and her friend rolled about laughing.

Next there was a scene in which a man was on his hands and knees being dragged through the streets by his wife by his collar, and in another it showed the silhouettes of another couple inside the house from outside. Saucepans, frying pans, anything that was going, were being thrown at him while he was busy ducking, sometimes only avoiding the missile by a quarter of an inch. Eventually a frying pan came flying out of the window, breaking the glass and landing on the grass outside.

Patients would frequently roll into the Casualty Department in agony, but at times it would look like an easy diagnosis for the doctor; for example, it might look like a typical case of appendicitis until the patient said, "I'm suffering more than when I had my appendix out". It always annoyed Jessica when people said, "It was only an appendicitis" when she had seen so many complications. Twice a patient had said with great confidence, 'I'm not pregnant, I've had my tubes tied,' but then it turned out that she was pregnant. The tubes had come undone. After that the doctors started cutting them.

Jessica was then put on to a medical ward. They had diabetics who would sometimes go into a coma, regardless of how sensible they were, how much they kept to their diet. But on this ward they had a diabetic who was an absolute fool, who wouldn't begin to try to keep to his diet, and the ward sister was fed up when another diabetic came in who was just the same. Sister was very unlucky to have two of them at the same time. One of them said to Jessica, "She's one of the old school, is she?" He did not understand. Jessica knew she would have to tell the ward sister he'd said this, that he had no intention of taking any notice of anything she'd said, because they could be sued if anything went wrong. She would have to pluck up courage to tell someone senior a patient had said this, for this sister was a woman who she had to practically salute. However, it came to no surprise to Sister, and she took it very quietly. "He thinks I'm a complete idiot, doesn't he?" she said, and Jessica just mumbled "Yes".

There was another problem – there were people around who wouldn't accept a diabetic's condition. They would say to them "Have a scone, there's no sugar in them". They did not accept that they were not to have such food. They would contradict what every diabetic specialist says. One diabetic said, "You'll find out when you wake up in the ambulance that there was sugar in the scones."

On the eye ward, some people could be stupid. They would lose their sight if they didn't put their drops into their eyes, yet some of them would not do it. One man had already lost the sight in one eye. The doctor warned him, and the patient said he always used the drops, but after the doctor had gone he turned to the man in the next bed and said he wasn't taking them. "Why should I?" he said. He had just been told why – that he would lose his sight if he didn't. He then said that he hadn't got time. So what he was doing with his time that was more important than stopping himself going blind?

While still on the medical ward they had a lot of overdose patients coming in. There were two kinds – those who meant to kill themselves and those who didn't. It wasn't unusual for the ones who hadn't meant to kill themselves to succeed, while the ones who had meant to die were brought round.

They had a lot of men with business problems. She wondered if they had tried to kill themselves because they had discovered that in a crisis some people did not care about you. There was one who had owned a small hotel, not much more than a large house, and the police had caught the staff going out the back way stealing things. Yet they had pretended to be so sympathetic towards him when he said how afraid he was that he might go bankrupt. Jessica's job was just to help bring them round. She didn't see them afterwards or go into why they had done it – a psychiatrist would come to see them about all that.

They also had a lot of men with heart disease who could drop dead on the ward in front of everyone. They would try to revive them with cardiac resuscitation, but she never saw a case where they had any success. She thought it was very bad for other patients with bad hearts as they must have wondered if it was going to be their turn next, and sometimes it was. In those days it was far more accepted as something that just happened. There was not nearly so much talk about prevention.

She worked in a clinic for venereal disease, and was surprised at the number of homosexuals who were getting it. She didn't even know that a homosexual could get these diseases and was very surprised how many of them were about. Maybe she just didn't pick it up when they were around. She wondered why it was against the law, because they weren't spreading venereal disease any more than heterosexuals. She was later told it was believed that men who had a guilty conscience about their sexuality had made it illegal; they wished they could be like them. In fact, it had been said that this was the cause of a lot of "queer bashing".

While she was still working on the medical ward, Jessica began to believe in letting homosexuals get married, just so that they could have legal rights with regard to one another, especially if one of them was ill. It was dreadful that only the family had any rights, and they might be interested only in the money.

She wished they would legalize it, so they could educate people. Homosexuals would hear the most dreadful things said about them, through nothing else but ignorance, and it could do great damage. They wouldn't dare say so. You didn't know who you could trust. You might be putting other people at risk.

As regards venereal disease, she was taught in the classroom "This promiscuous society has got to go." The germs were developing resistance to the antibiotics. They were saying to the patients, "We're very sorry but the drugs haven't worked, you've still got the disease." It used to be easily curable, just a few jabs with a needle.

The tutor who told them believed the new contraceptive pill had a lot to do with it. It was making people promiscuous. Jessica didn't agree with the pill, even though she'd been told it was safer than having a baby. One woman on it had died of an embolism and a doctor had said he wasn't certain the pill hadn't been the cause. She was only 28 and it was very unusual for this to happen to such a young woman.

Jessica wanted to go on living in the nurses' home, but there was one good thing about living out, they couldn't come into your room in the middle of the night if they were busy and get you up. She thought about it.

She worked in theatre. Here she was on call a lot and having to get up in the middle of the night was something completely different, as it was expected. They had to do jobs like lay trays.

They came for her once during the day and she wasn't even on call. She couldn't understand it. "Go to theatre!" she was ordered. It turned out that a swab was missing and she'd been there when the operation had first started. It was very serious; if it had been in the patient it would have killed him. They had X-rayed him so they knew it wasn't, but it was still very bad that it had got as far as that. However could it have happened when they had taken such care, and how can they sometimes fail to find out until it is too late? Yet she had read of such cases in the papers.

Every swab had to be counted as it went in and out of a patient, two nurses shouting loudly that they had seen it, counting one, two three, and then it was put on to a rack for everyone to see. It was also marked on a blackboard. Yet sometimes a swab was still left in a patient. Jessica was quite sure she wasn't responsible for this one.

One day she walked into a room and found a doctor there with no trousers on. She shot out again very quickly. He had been changing into his theatre clothes. She thought it was quite strange that they could stand side by side all day long, seeing one operation after another, seeing one person after another completely naked, yet it was unthinkable that they should see one another not fully dressed like this. It showed how quickly culture could change according to circumstances. She was leaving in any case next day. She never did find out if she was in some room where she had no right to be, or if it was his fault and that he should have taken more care where he was when he took his trousers off.

Another time as she was going on her dinner break, she saw a very old man going out for a stroll in the pouring rain in his pyjamas. It looked so bad, although really it wouldn't be much worse than getting wet in the bath. It wasn't cold and he was well nourished, so his resistance would be high. The Matron was on her way to the ward to do a round, and she and Jessica both rushed to get him back onto the ward. Jessica loved it, for he was very busy telling the Matron that she was to mind her own business and asking her "Who do you think you are?" These were all things she would have loved to have said to her herself.

She worked with children for a time; the visiting hours for them were the same as anyone else, an hour a day. She couldn't see that not having visiting all the time could be doing the children any harm; they would so often be just playing with their toys. Much of the day they seemed OK and only howled when their parents came. But she learned in the classroom from the tutor that people were saying it did a lot of harm to separate children from their parents all day long. It was even being said that it might leave scars for years. However one father did say to someone, "You might be a nurse, but you're not a psychologist."

She then went to work on the geriatric unit at St. Thomas's. She liked to be with old people, had worked with them before, but this was something quite different, for there were so many of them. She hated it, especially when she wondered if she might one day be just one in a row like these old people. As people lived longer, the problem of managing them was going to get worse. When she read about staff brutality in the papers she could never understand why the outcry from the public wasn't bigger, because everyone had an interest in it. They would all be old one day.

The lifting was horrendous, especially at bath time, and she seriously wondered if it was going to damage her back. She had heard nurses saying theirs had gone very suddenly, although the problem had probably been building up for some time.

There was one incident Jessica would never forget. A patient was brought in very dirty and the patient in the next bed was going on and on about it, saying "My house is spotless, absolutely spotless". The nurses commented to one another what a lucky woman she was to be so satisfied with her own housewifery – not many people could say that. They also wondered if it was because she was never there and never did any work in it that she managed to keep it so clean, especially when she came to the bit, "You won't find a matchstick out of place in my house". Did she ever use them? The Matron who was doing a round at the time said to the sister "And how jolly uncomfortable it must be to be in there".

Then something else came along that Jessica found impossible. She could no longer live in the nurses' home. She couldn't stand all the red tape. At one time she had thought that living out would have been impossible, having to look after herself as well as a lot of old people, but now she was finding it impossible to live in.

The nurses' home at St. Thomas's on Shaw Heath had been such fun in so many ways, or at least this was how she would always remember her student days, but it was things like having to be in by a certain time at night that made it all too much for her. There had been a lot of trouble over one incident in particular. One girl, Joyce, had jumped down from a high wall and landed straight in front of the night sister on her way to a ward to do a round. All the nurses had keys to the nurses' home, it was getting into the grounds that was the problem; they had to come through the porters' lodge and the only other way in was over the wall. This was at the end of a little side street leading off Greek Street called Royal George Street, running along the back of Stockport College or another very short side street also leading off Greek Street called Mulberry Mount Street. The other girls who had been with Joyce at the time had stayed there well hidden and making certain the coast was completely clear before they decided to leap.

Jessica knew this was going on in another nurses' home, a house in Lyme Grove that belonged to the hospital, and when the television was stolen they had felt a little apprehensive. The police were coming to take fingerprints and the students realised that theirs must have been there, all over the windowsill where they had been getting in at night. Jessica knew she was quite safe as she hadn't been one of the culprits, but she still didn't like it. She felt it was taking away her freedom and she wanted to be able to come and go as she pleased.

There had been an incident outside the grounds that had shown that she hadn't been one of the offenders on one occasion. She had been present when the boyfriend of one of the nurses, who by the way was also a young off-duty police officer, had called across jovially to someone driving a car, "Oi, the pavement is for pedestrians, not for motorists!" It was thought that this young officer had had one too many, and it was followed by a deadly hush. The other two nurses, who were also saying good night to their boyfriends, realised who it was he was calling across to. It was the Matron. Yet she had done nothing that was in any way dangerous; she had merely driven on to the pavement when turning a car round. There was no one near who she could have hit. But it seemed that in any case, even if she had heard him she didn't care.

It was a great shame that Jessica felt she needed to move out, for there was such a lot going for living in, especially if you had an exam coming up. They didn't have to look after themselves at all, just got waited on for everything at meal times, cleaning, no gas or electricity bill to see to and so it went on, but there were so many restrictions she felt she just could not live with it any more.

It was mainly the fact that she had to be in by a certain time that made her life so complicated, for although they could get a late night pass, they wouldn't always know in advance that they would need one, and in any case a late night pass only went up to midnight. They also had to get a sleeping-out pass if they weren't going to spend the night in the nurses' home, and they couldn't get one if they were going to be on duty at seven thirty next morning.

She found a small bedsitter for a very low rent in Heath Crescent, Davenport, with Cale Green Park at the end of the road. It was on the first floor at the back of the house next to the bathroom, looking out onto the back garden. The bed took up nearly all the room and the gas stove was next to it. There was no central heating, just a gas fire with a meter that she had to put coins into. It would be expensive and didn't heat the room nearly well enough. She would sometimes still be freezing and when she sat in front of it her front would be burning while her back was still very cold. Then she got herself an oil stove, which did the trick perfectly.

In the big room across the way, looking out on to the road, was a young woman called Clementine; she was 25, yet she looked more like 35, as she'd been ill. She had been given assurances that she would get her youth back again when she was better. Jessica found it rather good that she could go into Clementine's room whenever she liked, have a bit of space and lie on the big couch there, for indeed she was always made very welcome. Clementine very much needed the company, and somehow it helped her to get some of her self-confidence back again, for she had suffered clinical depression. She was a lost and lonely soul.

It made Clementine feel useful again that she could get Jessica's tea ready for her when she came home from work and sometimes cook her breakfast for her before she went out to work in the morning. Jessica needed it. She would work all hours, frequently doing a split duty. This would start at seven thirty in the morning and go on until noon, then she'd have the afternoon off and then go back at five and work until eight thirty. On days like this she could have her dinner at the hospital, then sleep on the couch in the sitting room, wrapping her cloak around her for a blanket. She'd wake up feeling refreshed and could have her tea at the hospital before going back on duty. Yet that didn't always stop her coming home feeling completely worn out, and she would still fall asleep on the couch in Clementine's room.

If she got up too late to have breakfast, preferring to lie in bed as she frequently did, she would take it off the trolley on the ward, slip into the kitchen with it and have it there. It was a deadly sin to do that, and there'd have been a very big row if she'd got caught, but she never was. It was meant for the patients, but they always had so much that it would be thrown away. It was quite noticeable that it was the nurses who had had no breakfast that were quarrelling.

Clementine had been an in-patient on the psychiatric unit at St. Thomas's hospital, but now she only attended the out patients, both places where Jessica had worked. Jessica would sometimes walk up with her if she had an appointment. They would also go for walks in Cale Green Park, or among the trees in the little wood opposite Heath Crescent on Bramhall Lane, and sometimes they would venture down Davenport Park Road and Devonshire Park Road, two wide but very quiet roads and a good stroll for someone getting over a nervous breakdown. They say open spaces help. They would then do a little shopping in the corner shop in Kennerley Road, which oddly enough wasn't on a corner.

Conveniently, there was a phone box nearby on Bramhall Lane. They didn't have a phone of their own and sometimes they needed to speak to someone. Yet it wasn't quite as easy as that, as so many other people also hadn't got a phone that there would always be quite a queue.

Chapter Nine

ABSOLUTE POWER
CORRUPTS ABSOLUTELY

Clementine had once been so full of life living in North Manchester. She had had her own house, had taken in lodgers and went to work herself each day, and then for no apparent reason clinical depression hit her. She went down to five stone and lost her voice, and for a while they wondered if there was something wrong with her vocal cords and did tests. It also seemed something physical, as she couldn't walk properly and was dragging her feet behind her; she was walking like an old woman.

She called herself a battered landlady and blamed the health inspector for it. She had been doing so well taking in lodgers, initially two men called Mark and Ken. Mark was dreadful, grousing away at her the whole time; nothing was good enough for him, so she told him to go. Ken left shortly after, so she was left on her own, and then came the reprisals from Mark. He had reported her to the health inspector and said that she was running a house in multiple occupation. She was not, as that means separate bedsitters with a non-resident landlady and she lived there. Neither Mark nor Ken had had a bedsitter; they merely had had their own bedrooms and shared everything else with her, the bathroom, kitchen and lounge. If a house is in multiple occupation it means the health inspector has a lot of power.

When he first came Clementine thought that there would be no trouble, that all she needed to do was show him round, let him see she was a single woman living on her own, and that there was no one else living there. And indeed there was hardly any furniture at all in any of the other rooms. However it was something he found impossible to accept, and she could only conclude that the drive to get control can be very strong, and false beliefs can be very fixed.

The next time he came round she had taken in two girl lodgers, students from Manchester University, and again they only had their own bedroom and shared the bathroom, kitchen and lounge with her. She'd been out at the time and one of the girls, not knowing anything about this, showed him all over. She showed him Clementine's room and said, "This is the landlady's". He made her feel quite nervous, and she was tidying up ahead of him everywhere they went. He told her, "Don't worry, it's the landlady we're after". That was true – maybe he should have said he intended to persecute her. It seemed he had been reading too many Charles Dickens novels, the way he judged her, and developed a phobia about it.

For the time being both girls thought that anything that was wrong before had been put right, but he did do something very strange. He told them where Clementine was living, and it was an address she had never heard of. He also listed all the things he said needed doing to the house, yet none of them were necessary. He wanted a sink and a gas stove into every room. This of course would mean it was a house in multiple occupation, and he would have a lot of power.

The girls and Clementine continued to live a quiet life, and then clinical depression set in. Clementine could no longer go out to work and was spending a lot more time at her mother's. This left the girls to fend for themselves, which would have been no trouble but for the visits from the health inspector. It became an increasing worry, and they would have to pluck up courage to tell her he had called.

Then they left, and Clementine went back to staying there all the time, but on her own. Her mother hired a nurse to be with her. One day when Clementine was out the health inspector came round. The nurse showed him all over, including Clementine's bedroom, explained the situation and thought that that was that.

Clementine then had to go into hospital as an in-patient, so the nurse left and the house was empty for a while. When she came out she got two other girls to be lodgers, but the problem of the health inspector went on. He told them Clementine was living at another address, one that neither Clementine nor her mother had heard of. Her mother telephoned the nurse who had previously stayed in the house and the nurse started to try to give her assurances by saying, "Honestly it's all right, I've explained everything to him, I've shown him all over, I've shown him her room," but she was interrupted by being told the inspector didn't accept it.

"Well what does he think I'm playing at?" said the nurse.

"It's a mystery to everyone" said Clementine's mother.

They decided something had to be done about him. It emerged that he had been round many more times than anyone had realised, and even when he could never find anyone in, sometimes in winter finding it in pitch darkness, he did not accept it that this was because it wasn't a house in multiple occupation but a house with no one living in it. It was an example to everyone, including the nurse, of how fixed false beliefs can be.

Something ironic then happened. When the lodgers didn't know how to tell her that he was still coming round, they feared it would make her ill, as she was already in hospital suffering from depression, they decided to tell the social worker in charge of her case, a Miss Firth, who they all had a lot of faith in. They wanted to protect her health from him, and yet he was claiming that he was there to protect their health from her. It was back to front.

And so Clementine, her mother, the nurse, the social worker and the two lodgers contacted a solicitor about it, a sort of glorified petition. The solicitor managed at long last to get it all stopped, but before he did another astounding thing came out about him. Clementine had telephoned the health inspector herself and he had said to her, sounding very fed up with her, "And when I sent you a letter registered post you sent it back and wrote on it, "not known at this address". It was an address that neither she nor her mother had ever heard of. He did not accept that she did not live there after all the many times he had been told, despite the fact that if he sent her mail there it would come back with this written on it.

It reminded her of the case of a very bad social worker, a Miss Fairclough, who refused to accept that a person had not been admitted into hospital under a section of the Mental Health Act. When she could find no record of it and no one knew anything about it, she wrote in the report, "Date and circumstances unknown", She did not accept that the reason why these were unknown was that it hadn't happened. Again, false beliefs can be very firmly fixed.

"But Clementine, you're all right now aren't you?" said Jessica, and she nodded that she was, and that she was getting a lot better. It was as though they were flatmates and had two rooms between them, the way they would go into one another's.

They would also frequently visit the woman who had the room behind the front room downstairs. She told them about things that had happened before they moved into the house. She was a sprightly 65-year-old and had a son who would frequently visit her. One night they came in together after having been out to dinner, and three men were lying on the hall floor very drunk. "Mother!" he had exclaimed "Just where are you living?" She had quite a time convincing him that she had just been very unlucky that he had seen this, and it was by no means a regular occurrence. However she didn't tell him shortly after this that someone had been in the place and stolen all the rent money out of the box in the hall that people would put them in.

However Jessica plodded on working with old people, thinking she should be more cheerful. There was an old dear, blind and deaf, on the ward who she would never forget as she was so cheerful despite the pitiful condition she was in. There was a tube by her bedside which looked like a hosepipe to Jessica, and they would talk down it to her. She would say to them, "Wrong ear, wrong ear!" Yet it wasn't often that anyone did speak to her. She must have been very lonely.

Then a doctor came round and ordered that nearly all the patients should be got out of bed, including some who were impossibly heavy. Although they knew the doctor was right and that they were being left in bed far too often, they couldn't see how they were going to be able to manage it. The ward sister said "We'll just have to do our best, keep a record of everything we do, and if we don't manage and get questioned about it, we'll say that it's physically impossible with only 24 hours in a day."

They began to keep a diary of everything they were doing, but it still worried the ward sister that a visitor might complain about a relative being kept in bed too much. Then there was a complaint, not that they weren't getting the patient up enough but that they were being cruel in making them get up too often. "Leave her in bed" the visitor said.

It didn't end there. During visiting hours the visitors would come into the kitchen and complain to them. With long-term patients there was more likely to be a problem with relatives coming into the kitchen. They would sometimes talk as though the nurses enjoyed it and were being sadistic, and nothing could have been more to the contrary. They had had their off duties changed so that they could do an early morning shift especially to get patients out of bed. There was nothing they would have loved more than to be allowed to lie in bed themselves and leave the patients to lie in bed too.

They would also get an extraordinary amount of interference, not from relatives but about patients who had no relatives. It amazed the staff that people could imagine that they would give out information about a patient to someone who was merely a neighbour. However years later Jessica wondered if they knew from the start that they would be told to mind their own business, but wanted to show the person was being carefully monitored. If so, it was a good idea.

It wasn't all criticism; some of the visitors were most grateful to the staff for looking after their loved ones and would give them little presents. One day a visitor came into the kitchen with a cake and said, "Could you eat this for me?" The nurses took it from her, thanked her, and after she'd gone they all had a piece each. It was a lovely cake. Then a while later the visitor came back and said, "Is it 'ot yet?" And they realised with horror that she had actually said "Can you heat this for me?" She had meant it for her old mother. They not only had to confess to her that they had done it, they had to make her realise that she dropped her aitches. It was lucky for them that she thought it was screamingly funny.

Jessica began to wonder just how confused some of them were, for although in many ways they seemed very with it, every now and again they would come out with something that wasn't with it at all. There was one woman who was reading a newspaper report about a man who had been sentenced to four years in prison, and she and another patient were saying "How absolutely dreadful, fancy not being able to go out for four years". Yet they themselves hadn't been able to leave hospital for many months, perhaps years. Maybe it feels different if a judge has sentenced you.

She would never forget the day President Kennedy was killed; it was a patient who first told her, a Mrs Passenger. Jessica couldn't believe it, and Mrs Passenger wasn't certain that she had heard right either, as she was hard of hearing. "We'll put the news on at six o'clock and listen together" Jessica told her, so they did. They were horrified when the news was confirmed, and Mrs Passenger fell leaning against the bed gasping, "It's wicked!" while a nurse went rushing out of the ward crying out much the same thing.

Another time she came on duty late one morning and a patient said to her, sounding very worried, "Do you know what happened to me this morning when these nurses were getting me up? My legs collapsed beneath me. They had to go and get a wheelchair to take me to the day room and I had my breakfast in there this morning." She was completely unaware that she was taken there every morning in a wheelchair for her breakfast. She hadn't walked for years. Then suddenly she came out with, "I hope I'm not going to become one of these cripples that never walks again."

"Just forget about it" said Jessica. "It was a one off."

She started working nights, but this time for more than just a couple of weeks to help out. It was quiet a lot of the time and she would sit in an armchair at the end of the ward with the other nurse and get on with some of the work needed for an exam. She always knew when morning was coming, because the birds would start to sing at the same time each morning and the light would start to come in through the window.

When on her break she would go into the office with a little portable radio and listen to it playing very quietly. One night she couldn't get it to play at all, so she gave up. In any case it was time to get back to work and on to the ward. Then when she was at the other end of the ward the radio suddenly began to work – it had warmed up and was now booming out a pop song at full volume, "YEAH YEAH YEAH…" She ran as fast as her legs could carry her to turn it off. The night sister must not hear that! But if she did, she would probably think it was just someone walking past in the street with a radio and never imagine it was on a ward.

However, about half an hour later the sister did arrive to do a round with Jessica. That meant standing at the end of each bed and saying how the patient was getting on. She found doing this at St. Thomas's quite easy as they were mostly long-term patients, but knowing them all at Stepping Hill when they kept changing could be difficult. She found it a lot easier after she'd worked on the ward a short while, and in particular to know the diagnosis if she had been there when they were first admitted.

On this occasion she and the sister stood at the end of one bed and the patient said to the sister, "Oh this nurse has had a dreadful time, a man came in here with a lot of drums". She pointed at the bathroom door and said, "He went in there and was banging away at them. This nurse had to race down the ward and chase him out." Of course she was referring to the racket from the radio, but the night sister had no idea of that. She said to Jessica when she had finished her round, "You know I had no idea that Mrs Forsyth was as confused as that."

Just as she was leaving the ward, she came face to face with one of the nurses living in the nurses' home, who had raced across in the most dreadful panic. A man had made an obscene phone call to the nurses' home. This happened so often that some of the nurses were used to it. It gives certain men a buzz to insult a woman, and a nurses' home is a place where he knows he can contact quite a few of them.

Something worse than that happened when Jessica was back on days. The assistant matron was doing a round, just to make certain everything was all right, when she found a waste paper bin on fire. The nurses were putting it out. She helped them by taking a jug of water from off a locker and pouring it on to it. Jessica had been at the other end of the ward at the time and was not aware what was going on, yet the matron said to her as she left the ward, sounding a little sharp about it, "And I hope you know your fire drill."

Jessica didn't tell her, "Indeed I do, I was there in the Great Fire of London in 1666".

These days when smoking is so widely prohibited it seems hard to believe that it could cause fires in hospitals in the early 1960s, but it did. Even during visiting hours they would have to go down the ward making certain that visitors weren't smoking. It was particularly dangerous if there was oxygen nearby. Once when the tutor was talking about it in the classroom, one of the nurses said, "The visitors, patients and nurses are not to smoke near oxygen". The nurse was very young and didn't know to leave it out about the nurses as the tutor would think that this would go unsaid. Indeed she did.

"What!" She exclaimed and the young nurse was indignant at being treated like an idiot, and said so to another nurse later. She had known a case where they'd had to move oxygen away for this reason. But anywhere else, for example the canteen, they could light up whenever they wanted.

Indeed patients were just lighting up. In fact it was a good way to get one old man to walk. A staff nurse would light a cigarette for him, sometimes her own cigarette, and she would say to him "No, you'll have to come across here for it, I'm not bringing it over there to you". Another patient suggested they should play the donkey and carrot with him and get him to walk a lot further with it, as the staff nurse had been quite anxious that he should stay off his back and not get a pressure sore.

Peggy came to see Jessica in her bedsitter. She had worked for a short while as a barmaid in a pub called the Stamford Arms in Bollington. She did have trouble with her arithmetic, especially when taking big orders when it was last orders and it had to be done in a certain time. There would be quite a queue waiting to be served. She doubted that she always guessed it right, although the customer never complained, maybe because they couldn't do arithmetic themselves.

She left after there had been a fight in the car park. She wondered why she let it bother her, for it was easy to stop, they simply turned off all the lights. She was in the upstairs bar at the time and hardly even knew it was going on, until a barman, keeping an eye on it, had shouted across to her, "Turn off all lights."

It was nothing like another pub she had worked in, the Bleeding Wolf in Hale, although that had only been while the landlord was on holiday. It started early one evening when the police arrived to take down the names and ages of anyone that looked under age. That was followed a few nights later by a lot of brawling at closing time, and although it was only scuffles they just couldn't handle it and the police had to be called. Peggy had to make certain she had heard right when the barman called across to her "Call the police", for it's a confession of failure to have to do that. There was another customer there helping out and no one knew who he was; he may even have been an off-duty police officer, for he seemed to know about dealing with this sort of thing. When the police arrived the yobbos all went running out of the fire escape and in the general free-for-all that followed in the car park, the police were for a moment frogmarching the barman across it.

After getting over all that, a couple of days later a fire inspector arrived to say there had been a complaint that the fire exit had been locked. When he came to have a look himself it was not, and it certainly had not been a couple of nights previously when the police had chased the yobbos out of it. They thought all this was going on because the landlord was away, and everyone was very glad to see him back.

Now she had a new job in a shop, but they weren't busy, so she had pretended to be ill and taken a few days off. Jessica thought how fantastic it was not to work in a hospital. They wouldn't know if you were giving all the wrong symptoms of an illness; you could tell them anything. However, you lost some pay if you didn't have a doctor's certificate.

But Peggy got the sack when she got back to work, because they did know. She told her father and grandmother that she had left of her own accord and they weren't sorry. They had been trying to persuade her to leave in any case. She said, "I thought everything over and decided to take your advice after all."

They had seen some of her English and thought it about time she went back to school. At the same time she could do something else, maybe history. She seemed to be taking a great interest in what had happened during the 1660s, so they got her to sign up at night school and to keep at it during the day. They felt she had left school too young.

Something else she wanted to do if she had time was to learn to drive a car. She hadn't got a clue about driving, and it was nearly all men on the roads. Living in Richmond Road was a woman called Molly Doreen, who felt very strongly about women learning to drive. She wasn't particularly into women's rights, she'd been a housewife all her life and thought that some of these women's libbers were over the top, so why she felt so strongly about this one was a mystery to her daughter. She couldn't see that it was men who were stopping the women from driving. It was the women's own fault. Yet it was Molly Doreen who got on to Peggy, as a friend of her daughter's, saying, "You must learn to drive."

Molly Doreen had also sat with another friend of hers called Helen Jason, who was 56, while she was learning, for although she couldn't drive she had bought herself a car. She was also having lessons from an instructor.

Helen Jason's husband was no typical man; he was an absolute horror, who criticized her the whole of the time although he never once went out with her. It wasn't his car and he didn't drive it. He would go on at her, "You'll never learn, so stop all this nonsense. Why don't you give in now instead of later? Think of all the things you could buy for yourself if you weren't having all these lessons." It would make Molly Doreen furious as she plodded on with her, sitting with her hour after hour.

Mrs Newton said that he should get a job in psychological warfare reducing people's morale, it reminded her so much of the war. The Germans would get through to the British on the radio during the air raids. It would sound like a sweet young lass talking, saying "Think of all the destruction and there's no need for it, we can come over and put it all right for you, we'll put everything together for you, so why don't you let us in now instead of later."

Mrs Newton had worked close to the Home Guard and knew how people were told they were not to listen to these broadcasts. It couldn't have been worse having it on while they were in the air raid shelter and bombing was going on above their heads.

Helen Jason plodded on with her driving lessons. She passed her driving test third time. But the second time she took it she did something very silly and failed on nerves. She later said she was going to discount that attempt as you couldn't call it a driving test, and that really she had passed second time. When Molly Doreen's husband saw the present Helen had given her, a very nice ornament, he said, "What's that? A farthing an hour?" But he was only joking. He was a very nice man and very happy that she had passed. It was his way of saying it had taken her a long time.

Molly Doreen thought so too, until her daughters started bringing home their young men. Helen Jason was promoted to top of the class. They had stories to tell which were worse than Helen's. They were very honest young men. They not only talked about how many times they had taken their driving tests but about some of their driving lessons and some of the calamities they'd had in them. Helen Jason's instructor wasn't ferocious and nor were the two examiners she had, for the one that passed her third time was the one that had failed her on her first attempt. When he did pass her he said, "You're third time lucky".

She realised later why the young men found the examiners much more pleasant than the instructors. It wasn't the examiner's car that was going to be smashed up if they made a mistake.

Peggy passed second time, and as she had had only two lessons in between the first and the second time she was able to say "I nearly passed first time." She found herself going around the house humming the song, "I thought the day would never come". She thought she'd never be able to drive a car, never mind take a test and pass it. She could not imagine herself being able to turn a car round, reverse or anything at all.

They learned how some people can delude themselves. One woman, Rena, was saying she had passed her driving test on 12 lessons alone and they all knew it was more like 112. Molly Doreen wondered if there was some connection between driving a car and having a feeling of power, as it wasn't like Rena to delude herself like that. When Peggy had to plod on with one lesson after another she was told, "There's nothing wrong with you needing all these lessons, but there's something wrong with Rena having a dream like that". But now all that was out of the way and she got herself a job in Woolworths.

Chapter Ten

LONDON AFTER
THE GREAT FIRE

"Is there any point in going to London now that Catherine's no longer there?" Peggy asked Jessica. They felt she had been a sister to them. But they decided to go, because they had some forlorn hope that they would see her.

Down and down the stone cottage steps they went, fearing what they might find at the end of it. They opened the door to find that they were in old London all right, but it was like a different place. The streets were no longer there; it was just rubble, for it had all been burned down. They struggled over it, having to take care to keep their balance at times. They did notice that there was some rebuilding work going on, and people were working hard at it.

Then they came face to face with Ginger. "Come with me" he

said. He led the way to a newly-built baker's shop. It only had one storey; they realised that none of the new houses had more than two storeys.

"Come inside with me" he said. He was quite noticeably shaken. "I have lost everything and everyone. I was a refugee living on the river bank until not long ago, and there were many of us."

"Well, you're building your life together now aren't you?"

"Yes, but things will never be the same for me again."

Poor Ginger, they thought, willing to do anything for anyone and this is what happens to him.

"I still have nightmares about it" he told them. "I wake up in the middle of the night thinking there's a fire, thinking everyone has gone, and it takes me a minute or two to remember, no, that was a dream. I get out of bed and think, I've got to pull myself together."

"What do you do then?"

"I light the fire, put the kettle on, sit with the cat and have a cup of tea. It takes me an hour or two to face up to anything, and then I see the daylight coming through the window and I think about the day I have ahead of me, but most of all I think about Catherine."

"What happened to her?"

"I'm afraid she died in the plague."

"I thought she went into the country?"

"She didn't go soon enough. She went to Bowdon, but she died there."

"Poor Catherine!"

They were surprised that although he was so upset by it, he nevertheless wanted to go on talking about it. He told them how it had all happened. He had been asleep on a straw mattress and was roused by Bessie, the assistant, who had been awoken by the thick smoke. Until then he hadn't realised that in the kitchen below hot ashes had been swirling out of the fire beneath the oven. He hadn't felt the draught that was coming through the open window above him, he hadn't smelt the smouldering of hay in the corner of the next room, but he certainly did now. He began to cough, his eyes began to sting, and through the office door he could see flames licking the walls. He could hear crackling in the wooden ceiling. He escaped with other people in the house through an attic window, all except Bessie. She was afraid of heights. Bessie was the first person to die in the Great Fire of London.

People were looking in amazement from the Star Inn across the way. The neighbours started moving their belongings somewhere that seemed safe, like a church, and then suddenly, without warning, the roof of the bakery collapsed. By then Ginger was running down the road screaming and banging on everyone's door "Everybody get out of your house, everybody run for it, it's fire! It's fire!"

The flames were being fanned by the wind, and the Star Inn soon caught alight. It spread into the next street and then the next. Horses and dogs as well as people were all racing along as fast as their legs could carry them. The flames roared away, sparks were being spread as the wind got stronger and timber beams were falling everywhere, sometimes across the street, providing another route for the fire. Yet no one could get the Lord Mayor, Sir Thomas Bloodworth, interested. When someone woke him up, he said, "Get an old woman to pee on it" and went back to sleep. There had been other fires which hadn't taken too long to get under control.

Ginger put his head into his hands and sat facing Jessica and Peggy. He wanted to talk about it but could only face so much at a time.

Suddenly a great ball of fire blew into the sky and showered everyone with hot sparks. Something had exploded. A big crowd jostled to get away, and continued to head as fast as they could to the river bank. A woman came rushing towards him. It was Betty,

completely hysterical. He got hold of her hand and they ran together
– it was run, run, run.

The fire was reaching everywhere and was now in the streets,
where wooden houses were joined together side by side. They were
very soon all alight and flames from the upstairs balconies reached
across to the houses on the opposite side. Betty's house had
completely gone. She soon accepted that and now she was running
for her life. She was a middle-aged woman with no family, but now
she had Ginger to run with.

There were people carrying children as well as valuables. Terrible
clouds of black smoke billowed over them as they reached the river.
By now the officials were beginning to take it seriously, realising it
was no ordinary fire, and the firefighters went into action, their carts
rumbling over the cobbled stones. There was a system of water pipes
under the ground for such eventualities, but in the panic to stop it
people were tearing up the streets, piercing pipes in so many places
that there was no longer enough pressure to make it work. In any case
there would never have been enough water.

There was a fresh wind blowing as they approached the river.
Timber was falling into the water, and it looked as though the river
itself was on fire. A few people went up to the top of the Tower of
London to get a better view, to find it was being spread rapidly by the
wind. Watermen who sailed up and down the river Thames shifting
cargo from one dock to another waited beneath the bridge in their
little boats. Meanwhile on shore, people were moving their
belongings to somewhere safe, only to find that the fire soon spread
there too and so they had to move them again.

Some people were very reluctant to leave their homes, and even
pigeons were refusing to leave their nests. They were hovering above
the flaming rooftops until their wings caught fire, and then they
would fall into it.

Many people were trying to escape on boats. Ginger was almost crying. "Some people who have a boat will only think about themselves in a crisis and how much gold there is in it for them. They will keep on putting the prices up."

Jessica and Peggy both knew about looting and knew that some people, if they hear that a shop has been flooded out, will go to see what they can steal, but this was the first time they had met anyone who had been so personally involved in it and who was so upset by it.

Ginger told them how people were shouting from the riverbanks "Rescue me! Rescue me!" He had got hold of Betty and told her she was going on one of these boats. She had cried back that she had no gold.

"I picked her up and pushed her on, and the waterman started coming towards me, as though to challenge me about it" said Ginger. "I shouted at him, 'That's where she's staying until she's safe'. I was ready to punch him, but I think he realised this, and although the boat was very overcrowded it rowed away. I didn't know what happened to her for some time but I did know that she didn't die in the fire. Then I heard she was working as a servant for a lady."

"That's all thanks to you" said Peggy.

"Yes, I know I should console myself with things like that."

"But didn't you need a boat yourself?"

"Yes. Not many people could swim. The boat could only take so many or it would sink. Then more people started getting stroppy as I had and were saying "I have no gold, but I'll chuck you into the river if you don't let me on to this boat.""

Peggy and Jessica couldn't bear to think of the people left on the bank, especially as it had seemed that one of them might be Ginger.

"It got worse, if such a thing was possible" he went on. "There were terrible clouds of black smoke above as though hell was in the sky, but I did just get away in time." He put his head in his hands.

174

"Oh, will I ever forget? Will I ever stop waking up from these screaming nightmares?"

He did get into a boat, and when it was out in the middle of the river the fire reached the warehouses along the river bank. They were stocked with inflammable goods and exploded.

"What more hell could there be?" Ginger went on. "It was as though it was raining fire, the heat was so intense no firefighter could get near enough to fight it. Everyone just clung to one another. The wind grew stronger and the boat was rocking dangerously. No one knew where they were going. Then as they sailed along they realised London Bridge was on fire. We could see it clearly. It looked like something malevolent, like the devil's work. It was indescribable. The houses on the bridge burned away, but luckily there was a gap in them left by another fire some time ago, so it didn't manage to get any further."

Meanwhile on land, people in the streets were using axes, ropes and iron fire hooks to pull down houses in order to make a fire break, but the wind was spreading the fire faster than they could work, so it soon caught up. People were trying to stop their houses being destroyed and the Lord Mayor wasn't decisive enough soon enough. Eventually King Charles, backed by the Lord Mayor, gave out strict orders, and soldiers and sailors were called in to use gunpowder to blow them up.

"But let's keep to what happened to you" said Jessica, so Ginger continued to tell his story. When he had first got off the boat he had had no idea where he was, he only knew he was very relieved to be back on the land and safe. There was no sign of any fire and the birds were singing happily away. Everyone in the crowd had soot all over their faces and clothes. He went under a tree, lay down and had a long sleep. How could he do that on such uncomfortable ground, while still so very traumatised? Yet he did.

He woke up feeling hungry, but still in a state of shock. A cart was coming along and he jumped on the back of it. The man driving it made him very welcome, saying he didn't want any money. He took him to where he wanted to go.

Ginger felt as though he couldn't thank the man enough. It made him so much less unhappy, especially when he thought about it all after, that there are some people who will do something for someone and for no other reason than they want to help. They won't take your gold.

He told them he had also been cheered to find that when word got about that a fire was on its way, some people rushed to get the sick and the disabled somewhere safe before they thought about themselves.

"But what about you, what happened next?" Jessica asked him, for they knew that somehow he had become a baker again. He told them how he had come back to London for a while and lived on the rubble left by the fire. Unfortunately, so had the robbers. They found it a good place to hide. They would pounce on anyone walking past and it happened so often that some men would not go near it without a sword. "I just couldn't take it any more, sometimes they would take off me everything I had begged that day" said Ginger. It was so typical of him not to consider getting a sword himself to try to defend himself that way. But he did move on to living in a tent in a field just outside London.

"I'm going to keep everything in black and white" he told them. "There are good people and there are bad people. For example, fancy sending a man to prison for debts when he clearly can't help it, he lost everything in the fire. And people who were living on the rubble where their house had once stood were still expected to pay rent for it! What sort of landlord is that? But then it was good people that got me back to being an apprentice again until I finished it and became a baker."

They noticed he had a cat with him, which had lost some of its fur. "It was shivering in the cold among the rubble" he said. Clearly it now had a good home with him.

"What I want more than anything is to have Catherine back again, but that's impossible" he said.

Peggy thought about her strange time-travelling powers. Perhaps she could somehow bring Catherine back.

"Ginger, if you yearn and yearn for something, sometimes you get it" she said. "I'll work on it for you." But that's all she did say, because although sometimes she had done such things, she didn't know how. She couldn't make promises.

They strolled very slowly back to the steps that led up to Willow Tree Cottage and on to the Devisdale, until they were back in Bowdon again. Peggy continued to work in Woolworths. The job meant running up and down all the time serving people. They were always very busy and she was always on her feet. Sometimes the girls would find money on the counter, and know it had been left by someone who had got exasperated with waiting, hadn't been able to catch their eye, so he had taken what he wanted and left the money. If a customer gave them a £5 note they had to ring the bell for a supervisor and she would come and change it for them. It was considered too much for them to do themselves.

One day she found lying on the counter a magazine about the history of Bowdon. She never did find out who put it there and it certainly wasn't for sale. In it she read of a Frances and Thomas from Bowdon who had lived at about the time of the civil war and who had eloped because their families wouldn't let them marry. No one knew what became of them. She realised it was Thomas and Frances who she had met in the 1600s down South Downs Road and that

177

Frances was the woman who was always looking out of the window. She wanted to be able to go back to the house, call up to her, ask her about it, say "What happened?" but she knew she would only be met by Mrs Lomax telling her to clear off.

One day she was told the manager wanted to see her. It was as though the Queen had asked for her. She didn't even know who he was, as she would see so many men walking about in suits. If you got the sack it would be the supervisor you saw, not the manager, so she thought something even worse was going to happen to her.

It was no such thing. Someone had been caught shoplifting and had goods on them which had come from her counter.

Speaking in a very gentle voice, he said, "Now I do know how busy you girls are, I have seen it when I'm on the shop floor, but you are still supposed to see to it that people don't do this".

When she told the other girls what he had said, they all agreed it was impossible, much as it would upset them when things were missing. At Christmas it was especially upsetting, as it was supposed to be the time of the year when you should show goodwill to all men. However, it seemed Peggy did get the message across, docile as she was, because after that they employed more store detectives.

There would be a grand feast in the canteen at Christmas time. It was noticeable that the girls who usually brought sandwiches in 'forgot' to bring them on the big day and would sign up for dinner instead. It was pointed out to them by the supervisor. "I don't think it's a very Christian time of the year to mention that" said one of the girls, although she did agree that people needed telling about convenient mistakes they make. Another girl said that as she worked all the year round she deserved the Christmas feast, even if she did spend the rest of the year having her own sandwiches.

Peggy, much as she enjoyed the roast potatoes and everything that went with it, would never eat a dead bird. There was talk of the headquarters of the Vegetarian Society coming to Altrincham, in an old Victorian house next to the Devisdale, and she hoped to be able to get some kind of job there.

One morning shortly after she had just arrived at work the supervisor took her to one side to have a quiet word with her. The management had received a crazy letter from the mad woman in Bowdon, the one that lived next door to the post office, and they all thought it was very sad. It was about Peggy and clearly she had written it in a terrible rage. It said she was running a brothel and an abortion agency from behind a shop counter in Woolworths, and everything she did and said was photographed and tape-recorded. It also said that Peggy was shortly going to be certified as a lunatic. The letter was full of blots, and clearly she had been worked up into the most excited state when she tore it out. The edges of the paper were very jagged. On top of all this some of the spelling was appalling, yet at the same time you could tell that underneath it all she was an educated lady. Clearly there was something very wrong with her. Apart from feeling pity for the woman no one was bothered, but it was just felt that Peggy should know about it.

Meanwhile there was something that did matter. Mrs Newton was finding it too much to run that big house. She wanted something smaller. She also needed the money, as with rising prices the outgoings were too high. She wondered if she should try letting. Peggy felt she should offer to go. However she had no need to leave straight away as a neighbour who had heard about it knew a young woman who was looking for lodgings. Mrs Newton had a spare room, so she immediately took her in. Her name was Jennifer.

Jennifer was 30. She never gave the true reason why she was there, or said who she was. She said she was a shorthand typist. She wasn't, even though she'd be off in her car every morning before eight and wouldn't be back in until after six. She took an upstairs room at the back of the house and loved it, not only because it looked out on to the back garden but also because she could bring her own furniture in and most landlords wouldn't allow that. She also had her own cooking facilities, or at least enough to make herself a cup of tea and some toast. She had lived in Gorton nearly all her life, but had to get away as her family had got mixed up in some sordid crime and she had a reputation to think about. She was a driving examiner.

She had been an instructor before that. She passed the instructors' driving test the third time, just as she was going to give it all up. She then got a job in a ladies' only driving school run by a Miss Smith. The problem with this was that with all the legislation they were bringing in about sex discrimination it was no longer allowed. However, Jennifer never minded teaching a man to drive, maybe that's why Miss Smith employed her. Yet there still continued to be blow up after blow up about it, and each time Miss Smith would teach a man to drive, saying that she never minded and that the men weren't coming to her. It was pointed out to her how very coincidental it was that every time a man asked for lessons she was booked up.

Yet at times she would be openly declaring what she was doing. For example, in the waiting room while someone was out taking their test she would go on and on about it, saying "I'm not going to teach a man to drive". This would be in front of other driving instructors, mostly men, and as Jennifer once said, "The examiners must be able to hear it too." That would be if they were in the next room, which they would be sometimes if a candidate hadn't turned up to take a test. But Miss Smith always had something to attack them back with. It had been alleged that some of the driving examiners were also sexist. She'd heard it said that all the young girls passed first time. In those days nearly all examiners were men.

"More women are needed for the job, they'd soon keep the girls in check" someone had commented. The trouble was of course that the men would then all be passing first time.

Eventually Miss Smith's discrimination got so bad that Jennifer had to go. It worried her what trouble she was going to get involved in and what lie she would be expected to tell. She then started training to be a driving examiner. It was no more difficult than being an instructor, and you just has to say yes or no. She realised of course that sometimes when you say "no" the candidate can cause so much trouble that the police have to be called, and the examiner can't get on with his next test. She'd been in the waiting room sometimes when this had been going on. She also knew that you get people turning up to take the test who can do little more than stop and start a car, they just did not know the standard needed, and yet it wasn't always they who would cause all the trouble.

If it gets dangerous an examiner can do a "walk back", that is tell the candidate to wait in the car where they are, and the instructor will come and see them while the examiner goes back on foot. Sometimes another instructor will see him and give him a lift.

Even if the candidate is doing well, a lot of the job can be boring, just sitting there, as they are not supposed to be chatting at the same time, yet sometimes they do. When Jennifer took her third test, they were talking about tennis.

"Don't come back beating one another up" the tutor would say to them as they went off to examine one another's driving, yet sometimes they would come back nearly doing just that.

Jennifer passed her test to be an examiner second time, and got a job straight away, the same day she moved in at Mrs Newton's.

She had a very bad first day and only passed two people. The rest were nowhere near up to test standard. The second day wasn't good either, until the last one, Mrs Jones, came along. She was 64 with grey hair, frail and extremely nervous. But weren't they all? Jennifer, fed up with absolutely everything, knew she should be doing better than this. She knew she should be smiling more, but decided not to bother as when the test continued smoothly she realised that Mrs Jones was very passable. Mrs Jones remained sullen, but Jennifer was sure it wouldn't be long before she got the wretched woman smiling. Soon she was beaming all over her face – she had passed first time.

The third day went splendidly, and she passed nearly all the candidates. On her fourth day one test was so bad that before she did a walk back, she had to physically intervene with the driving of the car. When she arrived home she lay flat on her back on the bed with the radio on. They were talking about the driving test. Someone was saying that some of it should be taken on the motorway. She had been dropping off to sleep until then, but now she was wide awake and screaming out, "Where are they going to get the examiners from?"

Next day they had to get the police in, as someone who hadn't passed caused so much trouble the examiner couldn't get on with the next test and the person who had paid him to take him was complaining. The examiner was called Mr Edge and was very experienced in this sort of thing. In fact since taking on the job he had changed from saying "swearing like a trooper" and was saying "swearing like a woman" instead. He said women had taught him a few new words.

Another candidate who knew the woman who was causing all the trouble said, "I don't know what all the commotion is about, she'll drive a car whether she passes it or not" and indeed, Jennifer was well aware that there were quite a few people driving who hadn't got a licence. It seems the worst thing you can do is to criticize someone's driving.

It amused her when a woman looked straight at her and shouted, "You'd wreck the place if it happened to you!" Jennifer didn't tell her how many times she'd had to take hers, followed by not passing first time to be either an instructor or an examiner. Later on during coffee break she found Mr Edge chuckling away to himself about it, for he hadn't passed every test first time either.

As the weeks went by she settled down to the job, but she would find it most frustrating if someone failed on nerves. One person had treated a traffic light, one that the workmen had put up in the road, as cross roads and gone slowly through it on red. She was in a complete dither. The shame of it all was, when doing so she had looked so carefully and showed how perfectly she could control the clutch and the accelerator and everything else. Jennifer realised that she could be quite passable, if only she could manage to stay calm.

Foggy days were the best days; if she managed to get in, all tests would be cancelled and they would just sit around having hot drinks and playing cards.

As more time went by Jennifer felt very alone in her room on her own. She started going out and meeting people. She would go into the Griffin at the top of the road, but she was finding so much revolved around drinking and pubs, and she didn't want to be always in a pub. At weekends she went to a night club with some girls she'd met, but she never drove. She depended on them for a lift. She'd pay them heavily for petrol and hope they'd oblige.

She didn't tell them what she did but said she was a shorthand typist. If they knew the truth she'd have to walk. She'd already had some experience of people being afraid of accompanying an instructor. If she was a passenger in a car the driver would start to tell her everything he was doing, as though she should have some say in it. Yet she was certain that the worst drivers were the back seat drivers and the best drivers were the ones who could ignore them. She herself was a very bad driver. She would go along the road screaming at them "It's ME that's driving this car, not you." And when she wasn't working she most certainly wasn't watching anyone else's driving.

When she was coming home from a night club she would crash down in the back seat. One night they were stopped by the police and the driver was breathalysed. Jennifer had had quite a bit to drink and was quite nervous, although none of them had done anything wrong. They got all three of them out and she was scared of being recognized. They were looking for something; maybe they thought there were drugs. They found nothing and the driver passed the breathalyser, so they let them go and Jennifer curled up into a ball on the back seat and went straight back to sleep.

After this she decided that too much of her money was going on drink, even if it was mostly at weekends and she had it under control. She would still wake up every Sunday morning with a headache, and one such morning she strolled up Stamford Road and into Bowdon Church. She had been woken up by the bells ringing telling her to go. It was a long time since she had taken communion. She sat at the back and hoped that her breath didn't smell of alcohol from the night before.

She picked up a book on forgiveness and wondered if she could really call herself a Christian as there were people who she would never speak to again. Why should she? They weren't sorry for what they had done and they didn't care whether she had forgiven them or not. She thought about it. A church sometimes does counselling, they must be trained, know that some psychologists say that some people will never change, yet they have something that overrides it. They say that everyone is redeemable. She felt that the church should make it clear what they mean by forgiving. She started to whisper about this to a girl, Sandra, sitting next to her. They agreed that at times it can be quite dangerous to forgive, in fact it may even be encouraging it if that person is going to do it again. Also, in cases like this, is it right to forgive if it's someone else that's going to be endangered? The conversation got so interesting that even when the rest of the congregation got up to sing, Sandra and Jennifer remained kneeling as though in prayer and continued to whisper about it.

After church they were invited into the curate's home next door for coffee, but didn't stay long. The curate's kids were driving them mad running around all over the place and leaving doors open with a freezing cold draught coming through, so they left.

Jennifer stood on the pavement waving goodbye to Sandra as she drove off. She had her husband sitting by her side and L plates up. "Oh please don't turn up at the centre to take it where I am" she thought to herself, as she would refuse to take her, saying she knew her. It would have been a shock to Sandra to see her there, as she had told her too that she was a typist.

After this Jennifer attended Bowdon Church more often and would also go sometimes to the church hall, next to St. Luke's at the bottom of Vicarage Lane in Bowdon Vale. They would have coffee mornings on a Saturday and sometimes jumble sales. She would see Sandra there, as she lived just across the road in Priory Street. Jennifer had always thought it was a mistake a husband teaching his wife to drive, as so often it finishes up with them falling out and Sandra and her husband Sam were no exception. In jokes it's the husband that is shouting at the wife because she's such a bad learner, but in fact it is usually the wife who is shouting at him, because he is such a bad teacher.

When they had first started going out together Sandra had thought that if anyone hooted at her he would say, "Now look at what a fool you are making of yourself", but it was no such thing. In fact he wouldn't let anyone hoot at her. She didn't know she was so precious. He would get absolutely furious. Sometimes she would say to him gently, "I know, you're right and he's wrong, he hooted and he shouldn't, can't we just leave it at that?" and at other times she would shriek at him about it.

But indeed it couldn't be left at that. One day Sam got out of the car and had it out with the man in the car behind, and when they got home Sandra had it out with him. There was to be no brawling out in the street. In fact she wasn't having him any longer as a driving instructor, and went to a school of motoring instead. She was never so glad as when she passed her test, as she could now go out on her own and everyone could hoot at her as much as they liked.

But Sam told Jennifer something that must not get back to her. He said, "The first thing you do when you teach your wife to drive is to how to reverse. Then if anyone hoots you get her to reverse into the front of him and then you get out of the car and swear point blank that it was him that drove into the back of her".

Chapter Eleven

TENANTS AND LANDLORDS

Of course Jennifer couldn't keep it a secret for very long at Mrs Newton's that she was an examiner and not a shorthand typist, but by the time it got out it didn't matter any more, and in any case she was leaving. She had someone to part share with in a house in Byrom Street, a little side street just by Hale Station. It amused her that as she was going she passed a battered man in the hall who was going to take her room, another favour that someone had asked Mrs Newton. "Seems good for business" Jennifer joked, "I'll get you a few more customers if you like". She meant some of the examiners she worked with and some of the shouting and swearing they had to put up with from women.

Peggy still felt she should offer to go. Then she was faced with another problem. She might not be able to find anywhere, for laws to protect tenants from bad landlords were getting very strict and they were coming down heavy on all landlords good and bad, so nobody was letting. It was ironic that for the same reason that Mrs Newton would now find it so easy to get lodgers, Peggy would find it impossible to find anywhere of her own, that is with a non-resident landlord. There had now become a big demand for people like Mrs Newton, that is, for anyone at all who would let you have a room in their home, and these laws did not apply to them.

They were now giving tenants in unfurnished property equal rights to those in furnished. This may sound fair enough, but it left the landlord with hardly any rights at all and very open to being bullied. Up until then it hadn't been unusual to hear someone say, "The landlord's very strict about furniture, he won't let me have any of my own" and people wouldn't realise why this was, but now they were changing it all. As a result scrupulous landlords would close the house down when the tenant left, causing a big problem for the homeless. It also created a problem for people who weren't homeless but wanted to move. Meanwhile unscrupulous landlords weren't deterred from letting because they would just break the law. They would make sure their crimes were difficult to prove, and they also knew how to intimidate the tenant. On top of this, even if they were found out and were sent to prison it didn't matter all that much to them. They might well be going to prison in any case for something else, and it would just mean that any sentences they got would run concurrently.

People were asking for a better balance, but some of the ministers seemed intent on going to even greater extremes. In fact one stood up in parliament and said to another, "It's my belief that your interest isn't in the homeless but to bring in a left-wing government"

Meanwhile, although some very good tenants did suffer, others were very bad and hypocritical with it. It seems that we are deeply indoctrinated into believing that it's admirable to care about one another. A bad tenant would say, even if they were planning on leaving in any case, "I'm going to be very awkward about going, I'm going to show my landlord he can't just throw people out like that". They would make the claim that they wanted to teach him not to treat anyone else like that. It wouldn't be any good telling them that quite the reverse might happen or more likely he simply wouldn't let it again and the place would remain empty, which would be very bad for the homeless. This wasn't their real interest, but just an excuse. The real motive would be to manipulate him, and maybe even jealousy played a part. Did they think all landlords had a lot of money? Sometimes they definitely did, and would say so.

Very often these flats would be let again, but to people who didn't really need them. A landlord would allow his daughter to live there when she could just as easily stay at home, and flats above shops would be used as store rooms and places for the staff to take their tea breaks. Sometimes a shopkeeper would live there from time to time himself, just to keep it lived in.

Although these laws did not include resident landlords and landladies, some of them were so frightened that they would not dream of letting. "One foot through the door and you'll never get them out" they would say, and that included those who lived down a side street in a two-up two-down and only had one room to spare.

Although none of this affected Jessica, she was having trouble with something else in Heath Crescent. One day she found a notice on the front door, "Please close this door quietly", so she always took care to do so. Soon after that when she was going upstairs the woman from the ground floor bed-sitter, Jo-Ann, came charging out towards her, saying, "This notice was put up for your benefit, we can hear you going up and down the stairs." Jessica was quite shocked at someone shouting at her like that. She didn't think she had been noisy, but then she was young, and young people do have a spring about them.

189

When going out through the hall she would see bits of furniture in it, or clothes; she had no idea why they were there. She wasn't very observant and hardly took any notice. But then Irene on the top floor told her, "That's an eviction order!" She seemed to think it was screamingly funny. The landlord was throwing Jo-Ann out, the woman who had complained about her. In those days you had to have done something really drastic to be faced with an order like that, and even then they could only evict you a little at a time. It had to be your belongings first, then the furniture if you had any, and the last thing would be the bed. After that the bailiffs would come and take you.

Jessica told Irene how Jo-Ann had shouted at her, and Irene was furious.

"The cheek of it! She lies in bed and pays no rent, while we go out to work to earn money to pay ours, and she complains that we make a noise and says we are not to disturb her!"

Irene had already had her suspicions that it was Jo-Ann who had put the notice up, and so had some of the other people living in the house. Several of them had given the door an extra hard bang when going out. They didn't want this getting back to the landlord. They didn't know that he would probably have been pleased to hear it, and especially pleased that they were saying it must not get back to him. It meant no one could say he was harassing her.

Eventually Joanne was evicted and Jessica had her room. It was so much better, more spacious, looking out on to the road and being downstairs. Clementine had now left, gone back to her mother's, so Jessica could no longer go into that room.

But some landlords and landladies did deliberately harass their tenants. Mrs Newton had a friend, Mary, who was prosecuted for it. The council lost the case and had to pay out a lot of money. Mary said afterwards, "I think the magistrates are absolutely fed up with it." By this she meant they knew she was guilty. She had three indignant daughters in court – how dare such a thing be said about their mother!

Mrs Newton wondered how they could manage to act so well. One of them, Geraldine, said with great force, as though she had a lot of fight in her, "When my mother went rushing into his room to save his belongings, there was a flood coming in, he was saying that it was her who caused it". But Mrs Newton knew very well what her mother had done and that it was Geraldine who had shown her how to do it.

"Then" said Geraldine, still faking anger, "Jim Pimlott got into the witness box and HE began to speak!" He had been there to stick up for Mary, the landlady. Mrs Newton was quite surprised, not so much at the lies he could tell but at the lies some people could tell on oath. He'd go to prison if he was found out. He managed to tell so many that he must have prepared it very well. When he left the witness box he marched away as though indignant at the things that had been suggested about Mary. He could act a lie, as well as tell it. Although it was sometimes in the papers about landlords going to prison for harassment, they wondered how many more of them were getting away with it.

When Jessica finished her SEN training, she wanted to come back to live in Bowdon. Mrs Newton wanted her back. She knew she wouldn't be able to find anywhere to live, so she forgot all ideas of selling her house, saying instead her door was always open. Jessica had intended to get a job in an old people's home, but she got one very quickly in a maternity hospital instead, Southfields, on the corner of Richmond Road and Langham Road. It had been there some time, two big houses knocked into one and converted. A lot of people could say they had been born in Bowdon.

She didn't have to stay at Mrs Newton's, as she was able to live in there for a while and had a room at the top of the house. There were two other nurses living there, one of them being the Matron and the other an Irish midwife. She didn't get on with the Matron at all, and she was known by the staff as "The Queen" They would always refer to her that way, maybe because she had started there on the day of the Coronation, but Jessica had her suspicions. She wondered if her queenly manner also had something to do with it. They had joined with Wythenshawe Hospital as a part of the group, which meant that she now had a boss. A nursing officer would come from time to time and see how she was managing.

There was also an auxiliary living there from Thailand, a young and beautiful woman who was never without a boyfriend. She couldn't speak English very well, so Jessica would sit with her sometimes in the evening in the sitting room helping her with this.

There were no cooking facilities, but they could always go downstairs at meal times and buy themselves a full meal for very little.

Most of the births were pretty straightforward, and only once was a baby delivered out in the street by the woman's husband. He hadn't managed to get her there on time.

Some of the midwives needed reminding that there were other things that could be delivered as well as babies. When one of them got home one night, a neighbour had taken a parcel in for her and then went to tell her "There's been a delivery at your house today". She nearly exclaimed, "Oh there hasn't been, has there?"

In those days you couldn't know if it was going to be a boy or a girl before a birth, and sometimes not even if it was going to be twins. One man had a surprise – first he was told he had a girl, then shortly after that that there was also a boy. He spent the rest of the day walking around the place with a big grin on his face and phoning everyone up.

Jessica moved on when the house closed down later, to be

converted into flats. They moved to Sinderland Road in Broadheath, she could have gone with them, and in a way she wished she had. The work was so easy and she didn't come home exhausted. There was also much less stress to it, as she especially realised a lot later on when she read something about another hospital in the papers. An instrument had been left inside a patient. The staff should be making certain this didn't happen in theatre as well as not leaving swabs in people. In this case the man had been at the airport, wanted to board a plane, but everywhere he went buzzers were going off. They checked his luggage and his pockets, but couldn't find anything. They checked all his clothes until he had nothing on. He was stark naked when they made him walk through a checkpoint, and the buzzer still went off. It was only after this that it emerged that he had an instrument inside him.

When she was working at Southfields Jessica became concerned about the problem of people getting the wrong baby. She was reading in the papers about mix-ups in nurseries, parents taking home the wrong baby and not finding out until the child was well grown. One couple were told after the real mother was dead, and then the child died. She was buried with the mother who had never known her. It had always made Jessica very careful always to put the baby back into the right cot and to keep checking the name on the armband. She felt they should wear their own clothes. Forever after she would tell anyone expecting a baby, don't mess about with pretty manners, you tell people how to do their job. When the bracelet is put on, you check it has the right name on it, and then when they cut it off because you're taking the baby home, check it to make certain it's got your child's name on it.

As a mistake like that would be very difficult to make, she did wonder sometimes if it had been made on purpose. Even then it wouldn't be easy to do, but evil people will find a way to do anything.

She also knew how people who get the sack can seek revenge. It crossed her mind that it might be someone who was working their notice. It may seem strange, but it would be an explanation.

In another case a child's adoptive mother had died when she was 12. Her adoptive father was struggling to bring her up on his own; they were poor working people. Then he discovered that she was really the daughter of a middle-class couple living in a moneyed area not all that far away. Neither of them had moved since the birth of their daughter. All three parents said they wanted them both, and as the daughters were now both 12, up to a point they could both have them.

Next Jessica got a job in a "hotel" called Chesham Place on the corner of Chesham Place and Stamford Road It was two houses knocked into one and very convenient, as it was so near to where she lived at Mrs Newton's, and although it's official title was "hotel" it was far more like a nursing home. All of the "guests" were long term, lived there, were elderly and needed nursing care. Things ran smoothly most of the time, although she came in one morning to find that one of the residents had dialled 999 in the middle of the night and said that the place was being burgled. Amelia Jackson, the young night nurse, caught him doing it and tried to explain to the police it was just a confused old man. "But he wasn't too confused to dial 999" they said, and turned up at the place to see what was going on. Jessica thought that that was the end of that, until she had to work one night herself. In the middle of it there was a knock on the door and when she went to it there was a young police officer standing there. "Is Amelia not here?" he said awkwardly.

"She left some time ago" said Jessica. She realised then that ever since this incident they had been seeing one another, and Amelia hadn't told him she was leaving.

Although Jessica didn't officially live there you could almost say she did. She had a room in the cellar which had been converted into a very comfortable bedroom which she could use whenever she liked, and she even at times kept some of her clothes in the cupboard there. She also had all her meals there.

Mrs Newton heard about another young girl, Charmaine, who was desperate for somewhere to live. She was a real hard worker who worked with Peggy in Woolworths. The family background was dreadful, the mother not taking her side against the father when he was clearly not normal. Maybe she was one of those women who won't leave a man and will sacrifice everything for him. It was amazing that Charmaine had managed to survive it. She struck everyone as being an average, nice person.

She had managed to get a bedsitter in Oxford Road in Altrincham, not far from the railway station, but one of the men in the other rooms couldn't keep his hands to himself. She was afraid even to have a bath. Late one night he knocked on her door and when she called out, "What do you want?" he said it could wait until the morning. When she asked him again next morning he denied he had done it. She found it weird. He knew she was vulnerable, that she had no one, and that it would be very difficult for her to find anywhere else to live.

But she did find somewhere; she took up residence at Mrs Newton's. Jessica was especially sympathetic when she heard about it. She knew how sick some of these men can be, but she also knew that not all of them were like that and that there was no such thing as a typical man. When she heard about the sick ones, it would take her back to the time she had been living in the nurses' home and there had been a 'deep breather' on the other end of the line. She could just imagine this man being one of them. But now Charmaine was free. She was at Mrs Newton's.

She felt so free that she gave up her job at Woolworths and went to work in a record shop instead. She loved pop music, so it was a job she enjoyed. It was in the basement at Whites and Swales in Cross Street, run by a Mr White and Mr Swales, the Mr White being the one who had sold Mrs Newton her first television set and who later started up the Bowdon Hotel. She didn't stay there long and moved onto working in a clothes shop, but there was something that started to bother her. One of the other girls, Pauline, was helping herself to money out of the till.

She was afraid she might be under suspicion herself. One morning Pauline's friend, Anita, came into the shop, and Pauline said to her, "Are you coming out to lunch today?" and pointed to her pocket. There was a ten bob note in it. She'd pinched it out of the till. It worried Charmaine, but she had no need to worry. It was just as well Anita didn't turn up for lunch, for if she had have done, she would have found Pauline gone. She'd got the sack. She got another job straight away in another clothes shop, but was sacked on the first day when the references came through.

Charmaine got herself a boyfriend, Simon, a police cadet who lived just down the road in Langham Road. They would meet in the shed in Spring Bank, just at the bottom of Stamford Road. Then he had to go away to college in Warrington. She found it very interesting to hear all about his work, especially in relation to criticism of the police. It was all about their rough handling of criminals, particularly one man, Bert Lightfoot, who had crippled a police officer. A door had 'accidentally' closed in Lightfoot's face and left him badly bruised. Parliament was talking about the need to stop police violence; they were not to be knocking the suspects about. The same thing was said in the police station where Simon worked as had been said in Mrs Newton's front room, as regards the Bentley and Craig case. Officers who were colleagues of a crippled or murdered police officer should not be the ones to handle the suspect.

Then all the newspapers ran a story about a horrible murder in Birmingham at a women's hostel. A body without a head had been found. It frightened Jessica that some of the deep breathers would hang about such places. This one was especially eerie, as when the man was leaving after the crime he had tried to get out through a yard, and footprints were found everywhere. He had been on one side of the gate while another of the girls had been on the other. She had been aware someone was there but had not seen him. It hadn't frightened her at the time, although it was beginning to get dark. She had thought it was just someone who had decided to go another way out – people do sometimes change their minds. Because she was there, the man decided to escape over a wall instead. He wouldn't have killed her if they'd met, as he'd already had a thrill to last him a while, but who would feel safe with that?

They got the man pretty soon after, in Warrington. It wasn't too far from where Simon was in college. The man had gone home for Christmas and met a girl. They would frequently walk down lonely lanes together. He said to her once, "I can't let you go home on your own, I would never forgive myself if anyone got hold of you."

Of course she did not know he had committed the crime, although she had read plenty about it in the papers, nor did she know he had just come back from Birmingham. However, she did know that they thought the man responsible had left a bloodstain on a bus – a passenger had gone to the bus conductor and complained there was blood on a seat. They arrested him, but he had merely been in a fight and had been saying to his wife ever since 'It wasn't me'.

The girl who was murdered was unlucky. He admitted he had been hanging about outside the hostel that night, and then, just as he was about to go away, the girl walked across her room and he saw her. It turned him on. He managed to get inside and find her. That walk across the room cost her her life.

Charmaine would only see Simon at weekends, and though she knew he loved going to parties, anything if it was to do with drink, she did not know how serious his drinking would eventually get. She thought it was funny when he once told her how they'd all been out on a coach trip and they were all drunk. They had to turn the lights out, to stop the public seeing the police behaving in such a way. But the coach driver was sober, and they weren't on duty, so did it matter?

She got tired of him and also suspected he was seeing someone else, which turned out to be true but in any case he stopped coming round to the house so it didn't matter. It was a friend of his that had given the game away. He had been quietly humming to himself, "You can't be true to two, true to two, you can only be true to one", a song that was top of the pops at the time and Charmaine knew that people will sometimes quietly sing what they are thinking without realising it. She already knew of another case where a man had been whistling an army tune and it later emerged that he'd been jealous of another man who had been in the army.

Much later she heard that Simon had left the police and was working as a postman. But they soon had him out of there. He was keeping a bottle of whisky in his locker and taking sips of it before starting out on his rounds. In those days post would arrive very early in the morning and people would always have the same postman. He could have the same round for years.

"Thank goodness I didn't marry him" thought Charmaine, many years later when she was hearing of one mad thing after another he was doing. When people are drinking it can get as crazy as a Charlie Chaplin film.

One day Jessica received a phone call from the one of the girls in the nurses' home; the home sister there was running it like an army camp. One girl had had a phone call at 11.30 at night, and the sister had answered it, telling the caller it was too late. She wouldn't get the girl to the phone and wouldn't tell them next day who the call had been for. However Mrs Newton's was too far away, so as there was nowhere else to go, she had to stay in the nurses' home.

Meanwhile it got worse. One girl had come off duty to find her bed had been stripped. The home sister had said it hadn't been made tidily enough and that she had had to make it again. It wasn't all that uncommon in those days for that to happen in a nurses' home.

Mrs Newton then got a student in from Manchester University. Students didn't have so much difficulty in finding accommodation because landlords didn't fear they would never get them out, as they leave soon enough in any case. Even so, there wasn't nearly enough accommodation going around for all of them.

When the word got about that Mrs Newton let rooms, people would knock on her door and ask if she had any vacancies. They would sometimes say they were students when they were not. They knew their chances of getting somewhere to live were greater if they said they were students. However, the word got around landlords that they should check that applicants were who they said they were. But these people would be nice people, and even though they got in by telling a lie Mrs Newton would be sorry to see them go.

Then a battered woman turned up, a schoolteacher, followed by another one, because the word had got round that she took abused women in. It wasn't until the third arrived that someone said, "The house is full of 'em." Another person said "Your house is being invaded, Mrs Newton". Indeed it did look like that, but she continued to enjoy having them. They were nice people, and if there was anything she didn't like it would always be sweetened when the rent came in.

It came as no surprise to Jessica when one day another battered husband turned up. It may sound sexist, but he was put in the attic, the only spare room in the house and not a bad room to have. It was nicely carpeted and decorated.

Jessica went that evening with Mrs Newton to see her doctor. There was no appointment system. Like all doctors back in the 1950s and 60s, he had his surgery in his own home. The waiting room was in the front room downstairs and the surgery was in the back. When his wife came to the front door she was grousing away at them both, something she had a reputation for. They couldn't understand it, because they knew another doctor's wife who was the same. For one thing she had been vacuuming and refused to stop when told. The cleanliness of the place was more important to her than whether or not the patient and doctor could hear one another speak.

And that wasn't the only thing she'd go on about. Jessica couldn't see what the connection was; it seemed that one of the hazards of being a doctor was to have a wife who wouldn't stop nagging. Many years later she realised the answer. It went on more than people realise in all kinds of homes, but in a doctor's surgery it's more likely to be noticed, and more likely to be talked about.

Charmaine came in very fed up one night at ten o'clock. She'd been out with a crowd of young people and the whole evening had been completely wrecked by a youth whose language was dreadful. "That's a good warning signal for a woman" said Mrs Newton.

Mrs Newton had an old friend, Elsie, who had had dreadful trouble, because she had been bullied by her tenants. This seemed to happen to women when they grew old and were widowed, and their families had left home. She had converted the top part of the house into a flat. Some women in this position were bullied endlessly. They would have to pay the bully thousands of pounds to get them to leave, and even then he might not accept it. Some of them didn't seem to want a good landlady; they wanted things to go wrong so they could get control. That's what they were saying about fascist political parties.

It wasn't fair though, the way Elsie would go on and on about students, calling anyone who was unruly a student. One day she was having a good "isn't it awful!" chinwag with Mrs Newton and they completely forgot that there was a student in the room. In fact he was sitting between them and had to put his head back so that they could see one another. It wasn't until they noticed the grin on his face that they remembered he was a student. But it could sometimes happen the other way about. Sometimes tenants would be saying "Aren't some of these landlords awful!" completely forgetting that their landlord was in the room. It reminded Jessica how she once talked about nuns in front of some nuns.

Elsie was being prosecuted for evicting someone. He had gone abroad and had been away for some weeks, and before that he hadn't been paying his rent. When she found his room almost empty, she cleared it out, but she was told she had committed a criminal offence because he hadn't given her notice that he was going and there hadn't been an eviction order. She should have assumed that he was coming back. But it seemed unlikely that the case against her would go ahead. Every time it was about to start she got a doctor's certificate to say she was too ill to attend. And so she was. She had a damaged neck, because a car had driven into the back of hers. There was more to it than her neck; stress alone can cause a stiff neck.

But not all landlords were being intimidated by their tenants. One young man was known to be such a quiet young man and no one knew why, but Mrs Newton did. His landlady had given him the thickest ear he had ever had. He had a history of being noisy, and after his second noisy party she went round to see him about it for the second time, and then he was sent a solicitor's letter, as he was in breach of several rules and regulations. Even then it was doubtful it would be enough to have him evicted, but clearly he wasn't going to risk it. Maybe he just feared having to stand to attention in court while he was reprimanded.

She was not the only one who would refuse to pay them a large sum of money to go. There was another such case along East Downs Road in Bowdon. The landlord seemed determined to get the tenant out, a young man who was something like two years in arrears with his rent. When the bailiffs arrived to evict him he jumped out of the downstairs window, ran down the garden and jumped over a wall into West Road and then into a car and drove off. That annoyed a lot of people. They said, "He can afford to have a car but he can't afford to pay rent." They might not have realised that it would be a lot cheaper for him to run a car than it would be for most of them. No doubt neither road tax nor MOT had been paid, and very likely he had no driving licence of any kind, or had ever had any driving lessons or taken a test.

Mrs Newton was very upset when Brookes, the grocer at the top of Stamford Rd on the corner of Richmond Road, closed down. She was told the supermarkets were forcing small grocers out of business and that she had to live up to modern times.

Then there was more trouble. A friend of hers, Ivy, was arrested for stealing from a supermarket. She had done all her shopping and then gone back to buy something else she'd forgotten. As she was leaving with it a voice said, "What about all the other things you've got in your bag?" She hadn't kept her receipt.

The police were saying that since the supermarkets had opened up there had been a large number of women accused of shoplifting who had had clean records all their lives. Some people said that it was because they found the temptation too much with everything now out on display, but others disagreed. They said that if they had been opportunists they would have been caught before, and none of them had been caught before. Ivy was found not guilty, but she said she would never forget that terrible day.

Then there was another grocer on a corner who wasn't going to give in as easily as that. They put "no parking" notices outside his shop, so he put up a notice saying that any of his customers could park wherever they liked and he would pay the fine. Everyone said he must have some secret agreement with the police, and the whole of Bowdon knew he had been down to Altrincham Police Station and played hell with them.

His shop was near a school, and all the mothers would go in there to buy all their shopping when they came to pick up their children. Mrs Newton thought it was dreadful when it was suggested that she should learn to drive so that she'd be able to go to a supermarket instead. She downright refused. She hoped that soon they'd all close down and the small grocers would be back.

One place that was still there was Ormson's, a workshop run by a family with a big yard attached next to the Stamford Arms on The Firs in Bowdon. If you wanted anything doing you could always go there, and that included the lady next to the post office, who clearly had serious mental health problems. Indeed she could call them any time, and at times it could get very noisy. One day when she'd had decorators round she asked one of them if he could mend her roof. He told her he couldn't, as he was not a roofer. "Don't speak to me like that, young man!" she barked at him.

She went to see Mr Ormson about it, and he said later to the decorator, "What did you have to upset her for like that? I had to practically throw her out of here this morning."

There was also a mechanic that ran a garage called Scragg's who stayed on and used the yard next to The Stamford Arms on The Firs. He was like the village blacksmith and would train apprentices. He had a notice up in his workshop which said, "No job is finished until everything has been put away."

One evening just before Christmas, Peggy was walking along Stamford New Road on her way back from work. It was six in the evening and the only thing she wanted to do was to get home. Christmas is such a busy time in the shops.

She saw a young girl on the other side of the road walking along towards the station clock; she looked just like Catherine. Then she saw a man coming along in the opposite direction but towards the station clock, and he looked just like Ginger. It looked as if they were going to meet. They were both dressed up in modern clothes. Then a bus got in the way, and she couldn't see any more. She tried to cross the road, but there was too much traffic. By the time it had cleared again they had gone.

She had to go home and have her tea quickly, as she was going off out again that night, to a night club in Altrincham. She was glad she wasn't a nurse.

Jessica was still nursing but had changed her job and was now working at Altrincham General Hospital. Christmas was no special time for them in the 1960s and although there were celebrations on the ward they all had to work the usual hours. This was particularly so at Christmas, as it was an especially busy time. It was the time when diabetics roll in because they have eaten something they shouldn't and the time when ulcers perforate for the same reason and so on. And yet the patient is not always to blame. They put a drip up for one man and he immediately developed gout, which he had never had before. Jessica said to him, 'Well Mr Jones, this doesn't say much for us, they say it's too much high living that causes gout, so I don't know what we've been giving you in the drip". They both laughed, and busy as they were, she was able to go to a night club with Peggy.

As they were coming out at midnight and going along Regent

Road they looked inside a shop doorway and saw a couple snuggled up together.

"Catherine, is that you?" asked Peggy.

"It is."

"Did I see you earlier, meeting Ginger under the station clock?"

"Yes."

She and Ginger told the girls that they met there every night and were no longer like passing ships.

"What became of Frances and Thomas?" Peggy asked.

"Oh, they ran away and lived happily ever after."

"Well why is she always looking out of the window?"

"I think because she always wished her parents had blessed the wedding that they didn't have to do it in secret. She always wished she could turn the clock back, do things differently so that they had done, she frequently dreamt of being young again and having that chance."

"Well what about you now? You must come back with us as you used to and bring Ginger with you" Jessica told her, but clearly neither of them wanted to go. They were very happy together and told the girls they would never grow old. They would always remain in Altrincham, happy forever.

#0002 - 170517 - C0 - 234/156/14 - PB - 9781861513281